"Did you kn_____ssive eyes I've ever s_____ tently at Dinah.

"Well . . . I .

"You do." He slid one arm _____ ulders and lowered his head toward hers. "And the most kissable lips."

"I . . ."

"Which I'm about to kiss."

Thank goodness, Dinah thought, then wrapped her arms around Preston's neck.

The kiss was gentle, sweet and sensuous. It was a meeting of lips that ignited desire deep within them, caused their hearts to race, and heat to consume them both.

Preston drank in the feel, taste, the feminine aroma of Dinah. His body tightened, blood pounded in his veins. He wanted her with an intensity like nothing he'd ever known. He wanted Dinah Bradshaw, now and forever. With regret he tore his mouth from hers and buried his face in the silken cascade of her hair.

"Preston?" she asked softly, not understanding why he'd pulled away.

"As they say in the movies," Preston began, forcing a smile, "this isn't the time or the place. Ah, Dinah, I do want you, you must know how much."

The baby began to wail as she nodded. "Preston, let's go home. . . ."

WHAT ARE *LOVESWEPT* ROMANCES?

They are stories of true romance and touching emotion. We believe those two very important ingredients are constants in our highly sensual and very believable stories in the *LOVESWEPT* line. Our goal is to give you, the reader, stories of consistently high quality that may sometimes make you laugh, sometimes make you cry, but are always fresh and creative and contain many delightful surprises within their pages.

Most romance fans read an enormous number of books. Those they truly love, they keep. Others may be traded with friends and soon forgotten. We hope that each *LOVESWEPT* romance will be a treasure—a "keeper." We will always try to publish

LOVE STORIES YOU'LL NEVER FORGET
BY AUTHORS YOU'LL ALWAYS REMEMBER

The Editors

LOVESWEPT® • 418

Joan Elliott Pickart
Preston Harper, M.D.

BANTAM BOOKS
NEW YORK • TORONTO • LONDON • SYDNEY • AUCKLAND

PRESTON HARPER, M.D.

A Bantam Book / August 1990

ISBN 0-553-44050-0

For Ed

Dear Readers:

Dr. Preston Harper first appeared in *Rainbow's Angel*, Loveswept #114, in October 1985. Since then, the flow of letters asking for Preston's story has never stopped. To all of you who wrote, I thank you for your patience. For those who are meeting Preston for the first time, I hope you enjoy the event. And to all of you, my sincerest thanks for your continued support.

Joan Elliott Pickart

One

"I want to have a baby."

If the attractive woman in her early sixties was shocked by her only child's announcement, she gave no indication of it.

She sipped some coffee from her wafer-thin china cup, then smiled and mouthed "No, thank you" to the tuxedo-clad waiter who approached with a sterling silver coffeepot.

"That's lovely, dear," she said pleasantly, replacing her cup on the saucer. "If you want to have a baby, then by all means proceed accordingly." She paused. "Since you'll be making medical history, you might even be invited to appear on *Donahue* or Oprah's show. That would be splendid."

Her lunch companion blinked once in surprise,

then burst into laughter. "Mother," Dr. Preston Harper said, "you're priceless, and I adore you."

Elizabeth Harper smiled at her son. "I've known and loved you for all of your thirty-seven years, Preston. Nothing you say or do at this point could possibly cause me to have an attack of the vapors." She rested her elbows on the table and clasped her hands beneath her chin. "So tell me, brilliant doctor, just how do you propose to give birth to a baby?"

Preston shook his head. "I'm not going to *have* a baby. I *want* to have a baby. Oh, for Pete's sake. What I mean is, I want to be a father, have a child who is legally mine."

"Go on, I'm listening."

"Mother, I'm an excellent pediatrician. The children I treat are the focus of my life, and the majority of my emotional energies is directed toward those kids. You know that's why I've never married. I simply don't have time to devote to a family of my own."

"So you've said many times."

"I've given this a great deal of thought, Mother. If I cut back a bit on my medical practice, and quit covering all the time for all the doctors who want to be with their families without interruptions, I *will* have time for a baby."

"And a wife?"

"No. Believe me, I'd like to be married. I've wanted that for quite a few years now. But once I start dating a woman steadily, it quickly becomes apparent that it just isn't going to work. Some of the women want nothing more than the prestige of being a doctor's wife. Others have demanding careers of their own, and have no desire to have children. The list goes on, but the bottom line is that I've never found a woman who is willing to meet me halfway on the subject of combining family and work."

"She's out there somewhere, Preston."

"Maybe, and maybe I'll meet her someday. I hope so. But in the meantime, I intend to adopt a baby while I'm still young enough to fully take part in that child's life, not be a grandfather figure."

"I still say the right woman is out there and you should wait, but . . . well, I know better than to get into a lengthy debate with you once you've made up your mind. So, how do you proceed?"

"I'm going to start contacting adoption agencies as well as doctors I know. I already have a large home, and a weekly cleaning lady. Plus, you know Clancy, my favorite nurse at Martin Memorial."

"Of course. Clancy is a gem."

"She's thinking of retiring but keeps putting it off because she hates the idea of having nothing to do. Well, I talked to her and she's agreed to move into my house and tend to the baby just as soon as I get it."

"My goodness, you have been a busy boy. And you're obviously determined to go through with this."

"Absolutely. I certainly wouldn't be the only single father in the world. It's not that unusual these days. How would you feel about becoming a grandmother?"

"Delighted," Elizabeth said, smiling. "I'd like a daughter-in-law, too, but I'll settle for what I get. How long do you think it will take for our blessed event to arrive?"

"I have no idea. I'm going to start the process immediately, and I'll keep you posted."

"Preston, believe me when I say I'm thrilled over the prospect of your having a baby, but there is no reason on earth why you can't have a wife as well. Before your father died, he was in command of a multimillion-dollar corporation that kept him extremely busy, as you well know. Neither I nor you suffered any neglect because of the demands on his time."

"Mother," Preston said, leaning toward her, "a corporation doesn't get colic, or ear infections, or anything else, in the middle of the night. My patients don't schedule their emergencies between nine and five. There's just so much of me to go around. I can't have it all, so I've made up my mind. I'm going to have a baby."

"Congratulations, sir," the waiter said. "Would you care for dessert?"

Preston strode down the hall of his clinic, shrugging out of his sport coat as he went. In his office he glanced through the messages on his desk, then buttoned a bright blue smock over his pristine white shirt and dark tie. A smiling chipmunk was embroidered on the smock's pocket.

Leaning across his desk, he pressed the intercom button. "I'm back from lunch, Clyde. What's happenin'?"

"New patient, room one," his assistant, Patty, answered.

"Roger. If I don't return from battle, I'm leaving you my dirty socks. Over and out, Hank."

"Gotcha. You're a peach of a peach."

Outside examining room one, Preston pulled a file from the clear plastic holder beside the door and glanced through it. As he reached for the doorknob, a piercing wail reverberated through the air.

"The natives are restless," he muttered, and entered the room.

Dinah Bradshaw jiggled the screaming baby she held in her arms. "Jenny, Jenny, Jenny," she crooned. "Why are we crying all of a sudden? Are we so unhappy, sweetheart?"

"I'd say she's mad as blue blazes," a man commented.

Dinah snapped her head up at the sound of the deep, rich voice. Her eyes widened as she stared at the man who had entered the room.

That, she decided, did not look like any doctor *she'd* ever seen. The man was gorgeous. Tall and broad-shouldered, he had thick black hair and an incredibly handsome, deeply tanned face. Even with a ridiculous chipmunk on the breast pocket of his smock, he was the most blatantly masculine man she'd ever met.

The man, whom Dinah presumed was the doctor she'd been waiting for, gazed intently at her for a moment, then turned his attention to Jenny. "Hey, Munchkin, what's the problem?"

He set the folder on the examining table and took the baby, cradling her in the crook of one arm. Jenny wailed on at full volume.

"See this guy on my pocket?" he said to Jenny. "He's one of my best friends. We go acorn hunting together on the weekends."

Jenny stared at him, shuddered, then stuck her thumb in her mouth. Blessed silence fell over the room.

"We found an acorn once," he went on, "that was as big as my shoe. You would not believe what was inside that acorn when we cracked it open. It was amazing, Jenny, it really was." He shifted his gaze back to Dinah and smiled. "Hello. I'm Dr. Harper."

Oh, help, Dinah thought. What a devastating smile. It lit up his face, exposing laugh lines at the corners of his dark eyes and revealing straight white teeth that would be eligible for a toothpaste commercial.

"I'm Dinah Bradshaw," she said. "How did you do that? I mean, Jenny was screaming for no apparent reason, then you . . . How did you do that?"

"Trick of the trade," he said, then turned to open the file. "These Munchkins and I understand each other. It's probably because I've never quite grown up."

Ha, Dinah thought. Dr. Harper had grown up, all right. He had, in fact, done a sensational job of it.

"Jennifer Mason," he said, frowning as he scrutinized the single sheet of paper in the folder. "Ten months and one week old. You're listed here as her aunt, Dinah Bradshaw, and it says her records are on the way from Chicago. So, Miss Jenny Mason, what are you doing in Stuart, Florida, with your aunt Dinah?"

Dinah sighed. "I just returned from Chicago a few days ago, Dr. Harper. My sister and brother-in-law were killed in an automobile accident, and they'd named me as Jenny's legal guardian." She swallowed heavily and lifted her chin. "You were recommended to me by one of my neighbors, and I wanted to establish a relationship with a pediatrician. I realize Jenny's records aren't here yet but . . ." She blinked back her tears. "Maybe it wasn't necessary to come here today. I don't know. I . . ." She shook her head.

"I'm sorry about your family, Miss Bradshaw," Preston said quietly. "It is miss?"

"Yes. My sister and brother-in-law's deaths have been a nightmare, a terrible shock. But I have to put all that aside and concentrate on Jenny."

Preston nodded.

"I've become an instant mother," she continued, "and, quite frankly, I have no idea what I'm doing. I'm an attorney specializing in corporate contracts, and I know absolutely nothing about babies. I have my own practice, and I've taken Jenny to the office with me the past two days, but that obviously isn't a workable solution and . . . excuse me, I'm babbling. I just thought she should be seen by a doctor now, so that I have someone to call when the need arises. She wasn't involved in the accident, so she's fine. I guess. But she cries so much, and I don't know what's wrong, and—" She threw up her hands in despair and frustration.

He'd like to nestle Dinah Bradshaw in the crook of his other arm, Preston thought suddenly. Despite her severely tailored navy blue suit and her thick strawberry-blond hair pulled into a bun, she was a lovely woman. A woman who didn't deserve to have tears clouding her green eyes. He wanted to comfort her, sooth away her sorrow and fears, tell her that everything was going to be fine. But he was a pediatrician, and his first responsibility was to his patient, not to the new mother.

"Well, Munchkin," he said, settling the baby on

the paper-covered examining table, "let's take a quick look at you. We'll check your oil and spark plugs, and make sure your battery is running at maximum power."

Dinah giggled.

Preston glanced at her, and she felt a flush of embarrassment warm her cheeks. She cleared her throat and adopted what she hoped was a cool, professional expression. As Preston redirected his attention to Jenny, Dinah let out a silent sigh.

She'd giggled, she thought incredulously. Like a silly adolescent. She didn't giggle, for heaven's sake. Preston Harper must think she was cracking from the strain.

Her glance slid over him. He *was* an incredibly handsome man. He seemed to fill the small room with his aura of raw virility. He was just so . . . there.

But in addition to his potent maleness, there was something comforting about him, a soothing quality to his voice and manner that tempted her to fling herself into his arms and cry for a week. His big, strong arms would enfold her. He'd hold her tight, nestling her body to his and—

Dinah Bradshaw, she scolded herself, stop it this instant. Where on earth was her exhausted mind taking her?

"On to the belly button," Preston said, calling her back to reality. "Jenny, you've got all the proper parts, and everything is in working order." He took the stethoscope from around his neck and placed it on her shoulders. "Check your engine."

"Ohhh," Jenny drawled, grabbing the stethoscope. She smiled and jabbered.

"She's a healthy baby," Preston said, looking at Dinah. "I'll review her records when they get here to be certain her immunizations are up-to-date, plus see if she's had any problems that required a doctor's care. Is she eating all right?"

"Eating?" Dinah dug into her diaper bag and pulled out a thick book. It had at least a dozen strips of paper sticking out of it.

Preston frowned. "What is that?"

She plunked the book on the table and flipped through it. "I bought this so I'd have a fighting chance of knowing what I'm doing. Let's see . . . yes, here it is. The proper diet for a ten-month-old baby."

Preston stepped closer and peered over her shoulder. Lilacs, he thought. She smelled like delicate, fragrant lilacs. And she had a lovely throat that seemed to be calling to him to plant nibbling little kisses—whoa, Harper. He wasn't supposed to have wayward thoughts about the mothers of his patients. But Dinah Bradshaw wasn't a mother, per se. Well, she was, but then again . . .

"She doesn't like broccoli," Dinah said, "but according to this it should be part of her feeding routine. She spits it out as quickly as I spoon it in." She turned her head and nearly bumped noses with Preston. "I'll keep . . . trying . . ." She stared into his dark eyes, which were close, so close, to her. ". . . to convince her to eat her broccoli."

"No," Preston said quietly.

He didn't move as he gazed at Dinah. He decided she had the most beautiful eyes he'd ever seen, then he went on to memorize her features, one by one.

"No," she repeated, nearly whispering. She blinked, then took a step backward. "No?"

"What?" Preston straightened. "Oh, yes, no." He shook his head. "Look, don't make a battle zone out of mealtime. If Jenny doesn't like broccoli, then give her another vegetable. Babies have definite opinions just as adults do."

"But the book says—"

"Miss Bradshaw . . . Dinah . . . those books are fine for a general frame of reference, but for the most part you operate on instinct."

"I don't have any instincts when it comes to Jenny, Dr. Harper."

"Preston. You'll find that you do have instincts once you relax a bit, get over the shock of becoming an instant single parent. I doubt Jenny will suffer any great harm while you're getting the hang of this."

"Easy for you to say," Dinah exclaimed, snapping the book shut. "You deal with babies all day, and probably have six of your own at home."

"No, I don't have any children at home. I'm not

married. The bachelor part is fine, but I'm hoping to change my childless status."

"I beg your pardon?"

"Ohhh," Jenny said, waving the stethoscope in the air. "Ga. Ga. Ga."

Preston took the stethoscope from her. "Thank you, ma'am. I'll put this away before you thunk yourself in the head." He zipped up Jenny's playsuit, then smiled at Dinah. "I want to have a baby. Adopt a child."

"Really? That's very nice but . . ."

He picked Jenny up. "But?" The baby patted him on the nose.

"Well, it's none of my business, of course, but you must be aware of the fact that you're a very handsome man. I can't imagine your having any difficulty finding a woman to marry you."

"It's not all that simple, I'm afraid, so I just want to have a baby." He tickled Jenny's tummy. "A cute little Munchkin like this one."

"I see. Well, the baby you adopt will be very fortunate because you'll know exactly how to tend to her, or him." Dinah sighed. "Jenny didn't end up in very capable hands, I'm afraid."

"Hey, Dinah, don't be so hard on yourself. Kids survive in spite of the mistakes parents make. It'll get easier as time passes, you'll see. Do you have a crib for her?"

"Yes. I had her furniture, clothes, and toys shipped down here. I checked what she has against the list in the book, and I have to get her more undershirts. Plus, her toys need updating. Hers aren't challenging enough for a child her age. That's probably why she pulled all the pots and pans out of the cupboards. Her toys are boring her."

Preston chuckled. "I doubt it. Pots and pans are just plain old noisy fun. Right, Jenny? You bet."

"This book is written by experts," Dinah said, lifting her chin. "I intend to see that Jenny has every possible advantage."

"I hope those experts remind you in every chapter that a hug and a kiss, some cuddling time, a quiet lullaby, a splashing good romp in a bath, are important parts of a baby's day. Those books by experts have a tendency to get very clinical, Dinah."

"Dr. Harper—"

"Preston. We all need TLC. Aren't there times when you'd like someone to give you a hug, let you know you're not alone in this big old world?" He looked directly at her. "Wouldn't you?"

Oh, yes, Dinah mused, her gaze captured by his dark, mesmerizing eyes. Right then would be a perfect time for a hug, from this man. A hug, then a kiss, then . . . She was thinking nonsensical thoughts again. Drat the man, he was throwing her all off kilter.

She tore her gaze from Preston's and jammed the book back into the diaper bag.

"Well, I must be going," she said, aware that her voice wasn't quite steady. "We've taken up enough of your time. I'm sure you're very busy."

His libido was very busy, Preston thought dryly. Dinah Bradshaw had caused heat to pour through his body, the blood to thunder through his veins like a herd of stampeding horses. He'd like to volunteer to give her a hug. Hell, he'd like to do more than just hug her.

"Thank you for your time," she said, then held out her arms. "I'll take Jenny now."

Jenny leaned into Preston's chest and grabbed his tie in one small fist.

"No, no, no," she said. "Dada. Dada."

"Now, Jenny," Dinah said, "we mustn't be a naughty girl. Dr. Harper is not your daddy, sweetheart. Come to Auntie Dinah."

Jenny tightened her hold on Preston's tie.

"Jenny," Dinah said, "we aren't behaving like a little lady."

Preston chuckled. "*We* are behaving like a brat. Jenny, if you strangle me to death, I'll never be able to tell you what was in the giant acorn." He pried her fingers from his tie. "Ah, oxygen. Jenny, you come and see me again soon, okay?" He walked his fingers up her tummy and she squealed, a big smile on her face. "Here you go, Mother." He shifted Jenny into Dinah's arms.

"How do you do that?" she asked, frowning at him. "Oh, never mind."

"Look, when Jenny's records arrive I'll give you a call and let you know when you should bring her in again. Your home and work phone numbers are on the sheet you filled out today, aren't they?"

"Yes."

"In the meantime, give me a call if you need me." Now, there was an interesting idea, he thought. Dinah—the woman, not the mother —whispering to him that she needed him. . . . And if he didn't stop having sensual thoughts about her, his body was going to betray him and embarrass him to hell and back. Shape up, Harper. "Okay?"

"Thank you." Dinah picked up the diaper bag and turned to the door.

"Let me get that for you. You've got your hands full." He slipped past her and opened the door. "There you go."

"Thank you," she said. "I seem to be saying that to you an awful lot. I'll wait to hear from you . . . about Jenny's records."

He nodded. "Fine. Good-bye, Dinah." Their eyes met and held for a long moment, then Preston cleared his throat and shifted his attention to Jenny. "See ya, Munchkin."

"Dada," Jenny said, holding out her arms to him.

"We aren't starting that again," Dinah said. "Good-bye, Dr. Harper."

"Preston."

"Yes . . . Preston." She turned and strode quickly down the hall.

Preston leaned against the doorjamb and watched her go, not moving even after she had disappeared out the door.

Dinah Bradshaw, he mused. She was a beautiful woman, and an intriguing one. He'd bet she was a top-notch attorney, coolly professional and always in control. But he'd seen another side to her in the examining room. Dinah was also a nearly desperate woman who had been thrust into a role that was scaring her to death.

Preston was pulled from his thoughts by the approach of his assistant, an attractive, young black woman, who was obviously pregnant.

"Meditating?" Patty asked as she stopped in front of him.

"What? Oh, hi there, Frank. How're things up front in the north forty?"

"Getting busy. There's no time to snooze standing on your feet, or whatever it was that you were doing. Your ever-efficient nurse, Mary, is in room two with your next patient."

"Thanks, I'm on my way." He paused. "Patty . . ."

"Uh-oh. Whenever you call me by my real name, it means you want a favor. I'm set on automatic no."

Preston splayed one hand over his heart. "Me? Ask a favor of you?"

"Every chance you get. Are you finished with that file?"

"Oh, yeah, here. Let me know the minute Jenny's records get here from Chicago."

"Sure enough. Go to room two."

"Patty . . ."

She rolled her eyes.

"Would you cut that out?" he exclaimed. "I just wanted to ask you what you thought of Dinah Bradshaw."

Patty shrugged. "I spoke to her for only a moment. She's very pretty, in a businesswoman sort of way. She seemed . . . I don't know, uptight with her baby. Nervous."

"That's just it, it isn't her baby. Jenny's her niece. Dinah became an instant mother because of the death of her sister and brother-in-law in Chicago."

"Whew. No wonder she looked like Jenny was going to break like a china doll any second. I really didn't look closely at the form she filled out. Is she married?"

"No. All she's got is a thick book written by 'experts' on how to raise a baby. She's scared to death."

Patty frowned and cocked her head to one side. "Why are you upset? Jenny isn't sick, and her aunt is probably very intelligent. They'll be fine. Now, go to room two."

"You're a nag, Sam. Your kid is probably going

to start barking orders the minute he's born, just like his mother."

"Yep. Go. Quit thinking about Dinah and tend to Jeremy Jenkins's sore throat."

"I'm not thinking about Dinah. I was simply commenting on her. Big difference there, Morris. I don't clutter up my brain thinking about beautiful women."

"You're so full of bull, Harper," Patty said, then turned and headed back down the hall. "Room two," she called over her shoulder. "Now!"

"Bossy. She is really bossy," Preston muttered, starting toward room two. "And I have no intention of thinking about Dinah Bradshaw."

But he did.

To Preston's astonishment and disgust, Dinah's image hovered in his mind during the remainder of his busy day at the clinic, throughout his hospital rounds, and on into the night he spent alone in his big house.

He was restless, unable to concentrate on the television program he'd been looking forward to watching. He gave up his attempt to read the medical journals stacked on the end table next to his leather chair, staring moodily at the telephone instead. Hours before, he'd somehow memorized Dinah's home and work numbers.

At nine o'clock he cursed explosively and snatched up the receiver. Punching buttons with more force than was necessary, he drummed his fingers on

the end table as the phone rang once . . . twice
. . . three times . . .

"What? Yes?" he finally heard Dinah say. "I
mean, hello?" The sound of a wailing baby nearly
drowned out her breathless greeting. "Hello?"

"Dinah?"

"Yes."

"This is Preston Harper. What's wrong with
Jenny?"

"Why are you calling? Did her records arrive? Is
there a problem?"

"No, no, I didn't get her records. I was just
thinking about . . . what I mean is, I thought I'd
check in with you and see how you and Jenny
were doing. Why is she hollering?"

"I don't know," Dinah said. "Jenny, sweetheart,
please calm down. I've done everything the book
said, but she just won't stop crying. She keeps
chewing on her fist and—"

"Give her a bottle."

"She's had her quota of food and drink for today."

"Dinah, haven't you ever had days when you
were hungrier than usual? Had an extra snack in
the evening?"

"No."

"Hell," he muttered under his breath. "Trust
me, okay? You go fix her a nice warm bottle of
milk. I'll wait."

"Well, the book says . . ."

"Dinah."

"All right. I'm at my wit's end. I'll go fix her a bottle. Are you sure you want to hold on?"

"Yes, I'll be right here . . . waiting for you."

"Thank you."

Dinah dropped the receiver on the sofa and sped into the kitchen with the screaming Jenny in her arms. She laid the baby on the throw rug in front of the sink, cringed as Jenny's cries grew louder, and began to prepare the bottle. She sniffled, only then realizing she was close to bursting into tears herself.

The soothing sound of Preston Harper's voice had been her final undoing. She'd been pacing the floor with Jenny, reading and rereading the book of instructions, and then there he'd been. It was as though, because he'd been popping into her mind with disturbing regularity all afternoon and evening, she'd somehow willed him to materialize. At least over the telephone.

"Two more seconds, sweetheart," she said, watching the water in the pan bubble around the bottle.

Moments later she lifted Jenny into her arms, then jerked in surprise as the baby grabbed the bottle from her hand and stuffed the nipple into her mouth.

"Oh," Dinah said. "Well, we certainly are thirsty, aren't we?"

Jenny sucked on the nipple, her eyes half closed in pure contentment. Back in the living room,

Dinah sank wearily onto the sofa and picked up the receiver.

"Dr. Harper?" she said, settling Jenny onto her lap.

"Preston."

"Yes . . . Preston. Jenny has her bottle, and she's devouring it. I didn't know she was thirsty. The book said . . ." She sniffled. "I feel terrible to think she's been crying so hard for so long because she needed something to drink. How is a person supposed to know? She was suffering and—"

"Hey, whoa," Preston said gently. "She wasn't suffering. She was simply letting you know she wanted an extra snack tonight."

"But I didn't get the message," Dinah said. A sob welled up and she forced it down, taking a deep breath. "I'm sorry. I'm losing control here. I really do apologize. It was very nice of you to call, Dr. . . . Preston. I didn't realize that this type of checking in was part of your service."

"It isn't."

"Pardon me?"

"I check on sick babies I'm concerned about, but, no, I'm not in the habit of phoning like this. You, Dinah Bradshaw, have been very much on my mind through this entire day."

Well, for Pete's sake, Harper, he thought, where had that moment of truth come from? He wouldn't dare say something like that to most women he knew, for fear they'd start choosing their wedding dress. But for some mysterious reason, he wanted Dinah to know he'd been thinking about her.

"Well, I—" Dinah started, then stopped speaking.

She did not, she realized, have the foggiest notion of what to say. She was quite adept at sidestepping men who made serious overtures to her, since the focus of her life—before Jenny, at least—was her career. Her social outings were always under her control. Since meeting Preston, though, her mind had slipped beyond her command, flashing recurring images of him. This would never do.

"I certainly thank you for calling, Preston," she said. "It was most kind of you. Jenny is drifting off to sleep even as we speak, so I'll just toddle her off to her crib and—"

"Dinah?"

"Yes?"

"Did you hear what I said?"

"No. I mean, yes, of course, I heard you, but I'm ignoring it. If I didn't, I'd have to admit that I've been thinking about you, too, and—" Her eyes widened in horror. "Erase that. I'm very tired, and I'm blithering."

A wide smile broke across Preston's face. "I see. Well, I'll let you toddle off to bed with Jenny." He paused, his smile fading. "Dinah, where are your parents? Is there any hope they might be able to help you with Jenny?"

"No, they passed away within months of each other over six years ago. I was a very late in life surprise, and they were more like grandparents than parents to me. My sister was my only other family. I'm alone."

Not anymore, Preston thought suddenly. "What about friends?"

"Oh, yes, I have a wonderful circle of friends. I grew up and attended law school in Boston, then decided I was ready to escape the ice and snow when I was offered a job with a firm here in Florida. I've met many marvelous people in the five years I've been here, but, quite frankly, they're all career oriented, and not one of them has a family. My friend Charlene stopped by earlier this evening, but as much as she tried to help, she couldn't figure out why Jenny kept crying either."

"So it's just you and your handy reference book." Preston paused. "Have you started looking for a day sitter for Jenny?"

Dinah sighed. "No. I have to, I know, but the thought of leaving her with a stranger is terrifying."

"Why don't you let me see what I can do about finding you someone?"

"I really hate to impose on your time, Preston. You must be a very busy man."

"I'm volunteering. Give me a few days to investigate this, okay?"

"Well . . . all right. Thank you very much. I

must go. Jenny is sound asleep on my lap." She hesitated. "Preston?"

"Yes?"

"What was in the giant acorn that you and your chipmunk friend found?"

Two

"So, Jack," Preston said to the man sitting behind the desk, "as my attorney, will you represent
me in adoption proceedings?"

"I'll be happy to, Preston. Hey, I've got a teen-
ager you could have cheap. Hell, I'll give her to
you. Fourteen-year-old girls are very strange crea-
tures. I'm not certain I'm going to survive her."

Preston chuckled. "I'll pass."

"Well, I tried. I'll contact social services to get an
investigation started on you. I've worked with them
before on adoptions. If you know a doctor who
has a patient who's planning on giving her baby
up for adoption, I'll act as the middleman so you'll
never know the identity of the biological mother.
Any questions?"

Preston shifted in his chair and frowned. "This sounds awfully cold. I feel like I'm going to the market to pick out a turkey."

"Preston, this all has to be done according to the law, so there's no question that the baby is legally yours."

"I realize that, but . . . I don't know, it's hard to imagine all this when there isn't a face to go along with the word *baby*. We're talking about a human life here, Jack, not some commodity I'm planning on acquiring. Babies are people."

"My friend, teenagers aren't people, they're aliens from another planet. The day will come when your child hits the magic age of thirteen. It's grim." He shook his head. "Anyway, expect to hear from social services. They'll assign a caseworker to you."

"Do you think I'll have any trouble being approved?"

"The fact that you're single might make it a bit difficult, but there are positive elements as well. You have a good income, a house, arrangements made for Clancy to be there. It would be less complicated if you were married, but I'm optimistic. Single parents aren't that unusual these days."

"I know," Preston said as, once again, the image of Dinah Bradshaw popped into his mind. He smiled, remembering how she'd asked about the giant acorn the night before. He'd discovered that the cool, professional Dinah, had a whimsical side to her. He hadn't answered her question, but had simply laughed and said good night.

"Preston? Are you still with me?"

"What? Oh, sorry."

"I'll keep you posted from this end. You start contacting the doctors you know. Social services has an incredibly heavy caseload, but I'll do my best to keep them moving."

Preston got to his feet. "Thanks, Jack."

"Preston, why don't you just get married and—"

Preston turned to the door. "See ya."

"You're crazy, Harper," Jack called after him. "Babies are dandy, but they grow up and leave. A wife is forever, until you're old and gray and finally croak. A wife is your best friend, pal."

"Have a nice day," Preston yelled from the outer office.

"Dinah? It's Preston."

"Hello, Preston."

"How have you been the past two days?"

"Fine, thank you."

"Is Jenny there at the office with you?"

"Yes, she's asleep in her playpen right here beside me."

"That's good. Listen, I've talked to a nurse named Clancy. She's going to retire when I adopt my baby, and move into my house. If you and Clancy hit it off, she'd be willing to put in her notice now and day-sit for you until I need her. She's a great lady, the best."

"Oh, Preston, that's marvelous. I don't know how to thank you. When can I meet her?"

"Why don't I bring her to your place tonight about seven? Unless you're busy, of course. After all, it is Friday, a night when most people go out."

"No, I don't have any plans. Seven will be fine. I'll see you both then. You're a wonderful friend, Preston. Good-bye."

"Good-bye," he said, then slowly replaced the receiver.

Friend, he mused. Jack had said a man's wife was his best friend. That must mean a husband was a wife's best friend too. Dinah had said *he* was a wonderful friend. And what all these thoughts chasing around in his brain meant, he had no idea.

"Yoo-hoo, mighty doctor," Patty said over the intercom.

Preston pressed the button on the device. "You rang, Fred?"

"Earache, room one. Diaper rash, room two. Runny nose, room three. Time to earn your keep. The Munchkins need you, Doc."

"On my way."

And soon, he hoped, he'd have a Munchkin of his very own. A special baby . . . just like Jenny.

Dinah stared at the telephone long after she'd hung up, the image of Preston Harper dancing before her eyes. She was pulled back to reality only when an attractive woman in her late forties entered the office.

"Autograph time," the woman said. "These letters are ready for your signature."

"Thank you, Anne," Dinah said, accepting the papers.

"Oh, I'd better keep my voice down. Jenny is sleeping so peacefully. Babies look as innocent as lambs when they're asleep. But awake?" She rolled her eyes. "Holy terrors."

Dinah laughed. "Jenny definitely has a mind of her own."

"When Jeff and I were first married," Anne went on, "we talked about having children, but we were soon facing his heart disease. We had eleven wonderful years together before he died, and I didn't miss not having kids. In the dozen years since I've been a widow, though, I've often wished . . . well, it's too late now."

"Too late for a baby, Anne, but not a husband. You've said you've been seeing your accountant friend, Joe, for several years, and that he asks you to marry him at least once a month."

"And I say no every time. I've been alone too long, and I've gotten set in my ways. I adore Joe, but I simply don't want to get married again." She smiled brightly. "But then there's you."

"I wondered where this conversation was leading, and it's a familiar path. You're determined that I should be Mrs. Somebody."

Anne tapped one fingertip against her chin. "Absolutely, and you have a marvelous selection to choose from. Let's see, you're dating Richard-the-attorney, Allan-the-assistant-D.A., Phil-the-stockbroker, Raymond—"

"Anne, for heaven's sake," Dinah interrupted. "Do you really want to hear my spiel again on why I'm not even considering getting married for several years?"

"Yes, I do," Anne said, planting her hands on her hips, "because if you say it often enough, you just might realize that your stand on the issue is totally wrong."

Dinah sank back in her chair and crossed her arms. "Not a chance. When I passed the bar, moved here, and went to work for that big law firm, I put in ten- and twelve-hour days for more than four years. And for what? To be ignored twice when they selected new junior partners. Why? Because I'm a woman, destined to marry, have babies, and chuck my career out the window. So, I mustered my courage and started my own firm a year ago. I'm doing fine, but I have a long way to go before I'm where I want to be in my career."

"The men you date would understand that you're—"

"No, no." Dinah shook her head. "I take work home nearly every night, Anne. When I marry— and I want to someday—I plan to leave my work here at the end of the day and devote myself to my family. I don't have the time for that now."

Anne's glance slid to the playpen where Jenny slept, and Dinah smiled.

"I know. Jenny wasn't part of the timetable I set up for my life, but she's here and I love her so much. I'll adapt."

"If you can fit Jenny in, you can fit in a husband," Anne said firmly.

"No!"

Just before seven o'clock that night, Preston stood in the lobby of a fashionable high-rise apartment building. Clancy had told him she'd meet him there. She had a friend in the neighborhood who was down with the flu, and who would benefit no end from Clancy's homemade vegetable soup.

At seven sharp, a short, plump, gray-haired woman bustled through the front doors of the building, told the young security guard that he was going to ruin his eyes holding his book so close to his nose, then beamed at Preston.

"Hello, Preston dear," she said.

"Hi, Clancy. How's my best girlfriend?"

"Not counting my aching feet, I'm fit as a fiddle."

"Good. Shall we go? Dinah lives on the ninth floor."

"Snazzy," Clancy said as the elevator started up. "This is a ritzy place, Preston. I bet it's filled with professional people who spend all their time working." She jabbed an elbow into his ribs. "Like someone else we know."

Preston grimaced. "You sound like my mother," he muttered. And then he wondered about Dinah. Did *she* spend all of her time working? She shouldn't. She needed to take time out for herself, and for Jenny, and— The elevator stopped, bringing his whirling thoughts to a halt.

The ninth-floor corridor was carpeted in burgundy and lit by softly glowing lights. Preston knocked on the door with the number 920 woodburned into the upper frame.

Dinah opened the door and smiled at them, and Preston was convinced his heart did a medically impossible cartwheel. Here was *another* Dinah, he thought incredulously. She was wearing jeans— very snug jeans—and a green blouse that matched her eyes.

And her hair. Free of its restricting I'm-an-attorney-so-watch-your-step bun, it cascaded in strawberry-blond waves to just below her shoulders.

She was sensational. And his heart was about to leap out of his chest and land with a splat on the floor.

"Preston," Clancy asked, "why are you still standing out in the hall?"

"Huh?" He shook his head and stepped into the apartment. "I'm not. I'm inside. Hello, Dinah."

"Hello, Preston," she said, closing the door. "It's nice to see you."

Nice? she thought dryly. That was not an adequate word. Preston Harper in faded jeans and a blue knit shirt was more than nice. He was a knock-'em-dead sight to behold. A funny fluttering had begun in the pit of her stomach and her heart was beating crazily. Why hadn't he worn his silly smock with the chipmunk on the pocket?

"We introduced ourselves," Clancy said, "while you were sleeping in the hall, Preston."

"Dada," Jenny yelled, crawling across the carpeted floor to them.

"Hey, Munchkin," Preston said. He picked her up and held her high above his head. She squealed in delight. "How's my Jenny?"

"Dada. Dada."

He lowered her, holding her against his chest. She patted him on the nose.

"She's nuts about my nose," he said. "Clancy, this is Jenny."

"Oh, she's a cutie," Clancy said. "Such dark hair and eyes she has. I swear, Preston, she looks enough like you to be your own."

He stared down at the child. "Yeah, I guess she does at that. She has my coloring, doesn't she?"

"Dada," Jenny said, and tried to stick her fingers in his mouth.

"Why don't we all sit down?" Dinah said.

Good idea, she thought giddily. Her legs were trembling so badly, they were liable to give way any second. Preston was there, filling the large room with his magnetism, saying, "How's my Jenny?" and looking enough like the baby to be her father. Preston was there, and she was falling apart. "Would you care for something to drink?"

"Nothing for me," Clancy said, settling into a rust-colored easy chair.

"No, thank you," Preston said.

He sat down on the oatmeal-colored sofa with Jenny on his lap. His gaze swept over the room, decorated in warm earth tones with splashes of orange and yellow. The furniture was obviously expensive, as was the state-of-the-art stereo system, television, and VCR. A floor-to-ceiling bookcase, crammed with books, nearly filled one wall.

"Great apartment," he said.

Dinah sank gratefully into a chair. "Thank you," she said, hoping she'd managed to smile. "I've baby-proofed it according to the instructions in the book. I've put away the knickknacks, placed caps in the electrical outlets, and on and on. I'm not sure what to do about the books and the stereo, though. Jenny keeps pulling the books off the shelves and pressing the buttons on the stereo and television."

"You say no," Clancy said. "You let her know what's not hers to touch."

"But the book says that one mustn't stifle a child's natural curiosity. They need to be allowed to explore the limited sphere of their environment."

Clancy nodded. "I agree, but not to the point of totally disrupting the way you live. Jenny has to learn that there are limits, rules she has to respect. It's a lesson better learned early on, because it's part of life." She nodded decisively again. "Just say no."

"Ga, ga, ga," Jenny said, clapping her hands.

Preston smiled down at her. "May we quote you on that?"

"Ga," Jenny said.

"Oh."

"Well," Dinah said slowly, "it would certainly simplify matters if I didn't have to worry about the books, the stereo, and the television." She frowned. "But this is Jenny's home. She should feel free here, comfortable."

"So should you," Clancy said. "You're not going to be comfortable if you're waiting for her to destroy the possessions you've worked hard to obtain. You share your home with her, you don't turn it over to her. A married couple respects each other's personal possessions. Why shouldn't a child?"

Dinah pressed one hand to her forehead. "This is very confusing. The book says . . . oh, dear."

"Ga," Jenny cried merrily.

"Shh, Jenny," Preston said.

Clancy leaned forward in her chair. "Dinah honey, you're doing fine with Jenny. You're a good mother already because you have a bushel of love to give to that baby. With that as a foundation, the rest will just fall into place as nice as you please. Stop fretting about every little thing and enjoy your baby. Lord knows they grow up so fast, it's quicker than a blink of an eye. Love Jenny, Dinah, and you'll get that love back tenfold."

"Thank you, Clancy," Dinah said, blinking against unexpected tears. "You're very kind. Would you . . . would you be willing to be Jenny's day sitter here at my apartment? I realize you're moving to Preston's when he adopts his baby, but if you'd care for Jenny in the meantime, I'd be very grateful."

"I'd be delighted," Clancy said. "They know at the hospital that I plan to retire, and I'm already training my replacement. I have oodles of vacation time and sick leave coming to me. I'll wrap things up there and be available for you just as soon as I can."

"Oh, that's wonderful," Dinah said.

During the next few minutes Dinah and Clancy agreed on a salary and the time Clancy would arrive at the apartment in the morning. Dinah assured Clancy she'd never be late coming home.

With everything settled, Clancy wished Preston a pleasant good night, blew a kiss to Jenny, and bustled out of the apartment. Dinah closed the door behind her and turned to smile at Preston.

"She's marvelous, Preston. How can I ever thank you? I can't begin to tell you what a relief it is to—" She paused. "You're still here."

"Yes," he said, standing up with Jenny in his

arms. "Clancy and I came in separate cars. She visited a sick friend before meeting me."

"I see."

"Listen, Jenny's getting fussy. Why don't I get her into her pajamas while you fix her a bottle?"

"But . . . well, all right. Her room is on the left, down the hall there. Her pajamas are in the top bin of the dressing table. She wears two diapers at night."

"Got it. Come on, Munchkin. Let's get you ready to hit the sack."

"Dada," Jenny said. "Da. Da."

"Did I ever tell you about the whale in my bathtub?" Preston said as he started down the hall. "He was a great guy, that whale, told some of the best fish stories I've ever heard. I remember the time he . . ."

Dinah watched as the pair disappeared into Jenny's room, then walked slowly into the kitchen.

Just like a real family, she mused as she prepared Jenny's bottle. Mother and Father were sharing the job of preparing Baby for bed. They'd tuck Jenny in for the night, then . . . Dinah Bradshaw, stop it.

She plunked the bottle in a pan of water, turned the burner on, then absently watched the water heat.

Those had been ridiculous thoughts, she chided herself. She and Jenny were a family, just the two of them. Preston was . . . Preston. He was a good friend who had gone out of his way to help her. She was all set now with Clancy. She wouldn't be seeing Preston again except as Jenny's doctor.

Dinah frowned. She wouldn't be seeing Preston again? Why did a cold knot tighten in her stomach at that thought? Why did a wave of gloom wash over her when she pictured him walking out of her apartment, never to return?

She snatched the bottle out of the pan and went back into the living room just as Preston entered from the hall. He held out one hand for the bottle.

"You're going to feed her?" she asked.

"Sure. Take the night off, Mother. Don't ever pass up an offer of help when it comes to caring for a Munchkin. They're exhausting little critters." He settled onto the sofa with a pajama-clad Jenny.

What a lovely picture they made together, Dinah thought as she sat back down in her chair. It wasn't just because they had the same coloring and were both attractive, in their own ways. It was the unconditional trust Jenny had for Preston. And it was the tender, genuine caring Preston had for her. He was a big, strong man who wasn't afraid to allow the gentle side of his nature to be seen.

She'd never met anyone like Preston Harper before, she realized. It looked right, it *felt* right, to have him there, tending to Jenny.

Preston shifted his gaze from Jenny to Dinah.

Their eyes met, met and held. Slowly the atmosphere in the room changed. Sexual awareness seemed to crackle through the air like lightning. Jenny was forgotten as their breathing quickened, their hearts beat wildly.

"Ah," Jenny sighed, and flipped her empty bottle onto the floor.

Both Dinah and Preston started, then looked at the drowsy baby.

"She finished her milk," Preston said. Lord, Harper, he thought, what a brilliant observation. But at the moment it was a wonder he could string two sensible words together. Dinah Bradshaw was turning him inside out. "Shall we put Jenny to bed?"

"Who?" Dinah said blankly. "Oh." She jumped to her feet. "Yes, of course. I'll take her."

"Good night, Munchkin." He kissed Jenny on the top of her head, then stood and placed her in Dinah's arms. "She's just about asleep."

"That's nice," Dinah said, not looking at Preston.

She hurried down the hall to Jenny's bedroom. After laying the baby on her stomach in the crib, she covered her with a light blanket. Jenny wiggled, stuck her thumb in her mouth, and closed her eyes.

Dinah gripped the top rail of the crib and stared at the sleeping child. There was no reason for her to stand there another second, but—oh, Lord—Preston was waiting for her in the living room.

She'd felt so strange when he looked at her, pinned her in place with those compelling dark eyes of his. Heat had pulsed deep within her; her racing heartbeat had echoed in her ears. Desire had consumed her.

She shook her head wildly. She wouldn't, couldn't, succumb to Preston's vibrant masculinity. There was no place in her life for someone like him, for someone who evoked such potent sensations within her. If they had met later, they might . . .

Jenny sighed in her sleep.

Dinah smiled at the baby, then took a deep breath, lifted her chin, and marched back into the living room. Her step faltered slightly when she saw Preston, his back to her as he scanned the books on her shelves.

He was just so damnably beautiful, she thought. Forget that. She was going to hustle him out of there in five seconds flat.

"Well," she said loudly, "Jenny is asleep, and that's that. Let me say again how much I appreciate your introducing me to Clancy. Everything is under control."

He turned to face her, his expression serious. "Is it?" he asked quietly.

"Certainly."

"Is that your attorney voice, Dinah? So cool and clipped. Is that your lawyer smile?" He paused. "Okay, counselor, explain to me, a jury of one, what's happening between us."

Dinah's smile disappeared. "Happening? Between us? I have no idea what you're referring to."

"Oh, come on," he said, his voice rising. "You felt it a few minutes ago, just as I did. You've also admitted that I've been on your mind, and Lord knows you've been on mine. What do you suppose this is, Ms. Bradshaw?"

"It's nothing."

"Bull."

"Don't get nasty, Preston. I don't know what you're so angry about all of a sudden. So, all right, there's a physical attraction between us. That's simple enough to understand. That doesn't mean we're going to pursue it. You have your life set up the way you want it, and so do I. End of story. I'm making the necessary adjustments for Jenny, but I'm still moving forward toward my goals."

He closed the distance between them in three long strides, and she stared up at him with wide eyes.

"Very pretty speech," he said, "but save it for your contracts. Life doesn't work that way. Jenny was a little glitch in your program, but you've got that worked out, right? As for what's happening between us, you're going to chalk it up as plain old lust and go blissfully on your way. Well, I want some *real* answers as to why I can't get you out of my mind day and night. And why every time I'm near you I want you so badly I ache. I— Oh, hell."

Gripping her arms, he hauled her to him and brought his mouth down hard onto hers.

Dinah stiffened in shock, and instantly his kiss gentled to a soft, sensuous meeting of their lips. Her eyes drifted closed and her hands floated up to encircle his neck.

Preston, she thought dreamily. At long last, Preston.

Heat throbbed deep within Preston, as his manhood surged with desire for Dinah.

An eternity, he thought. He'd waited an eternity for this kiss. Passion swept through him like a flash fire out of control.

Good Lord, how he wanted this woman.

His hands roamed restlessly over her back, then lower, to her rounded buttocks. He nestled her in the cradle of his hips, his arousal heavy against her. A groan rumbled in his throat as he felt her press her breasts to his chest.

He deepened the kiss, his tongue finding hers, and savored her sweet taste. Even the lingering scent of baby powder was an aphrodisiac.

But he wanted more. He wanted to mesh his body with hers and make them one entity. He wanted all of her—the cool, professional Dinah and Dinah the mother. The frightened woman and the competent businesswoman. The whimsical Dinah who wondered about secrets in giant acorns. It would be ecstasy.

"Dinah," he murmured, his lips against hers, "I want you so damn much."

She wanted him, too, Dinah thought hazily. Wanted him with an intensity of passion she hadn't realized she was capable of. Preston aroused desire within her that was unlike anything she'd ever experienced.

He was so strong, and she felt fragile, protected, in his arms, just as she'd known she would. His taste, his aroma, his . . . everything, were hers. They would make glorious love . . . in her bed . . . down the hall . . . across from where . . . Jenny slept peacefully in her crib.

Dinah's eyes flew open, and she jerked her head back.

"Jenny!" she exclaimed, and drew in a much-needed breath.

"Sound asleep," Preston said, not releasing his hold on her.

"She's here."

He frowned. "Well, yes. I doubt she snuck out and went to look for a job. Dinah—"

"No." She wriggled out of his embrace and took a step backward. "Oh, dear heaven, what have I done? This is terrible."

"Thanks a lot." His frown deepened. "I personally thought those kisses were fantastic."

"Oh, they were, they were," she said, her voice suddenly wistful. Then she shook her head. "That's not the point."

"What in the hell *is* the point?" he asked, gesturing wildly. "I want you, you want me. We're two consenting adults with every right to make the decision to . . . Dammit, Dinah, it's more than lust. You must know that by now. There's something special, important, happening between us."

A bubble of laughter escaped her lips. Did she sound hysterical? she wondered. Dammit, Dinah? That rhymes. Sort of. Oh, Lord, I am getting hysterical. She took another deep breath, then lifted her chin. "Preston, I apologize for my behavior. I'm not in the habit of conducting myself in such a—a wanton manner. If I led you to believe that I was agreeing to . . . I really do apologize."

"Would you knock that off? You get a really snooty sound to your voice when you switch to your attorney mode."

"Well, excuse me," she exclaimed, planting her hands on her hips.

"No, I won't excuse you. You wanted me, Dinah Bradshaw, and then you called a halt. Why?"

"Because, you schnook, I don't have room in my life for you, for us, for"—she waved one hand in the air—"whatever this is that you claim is more than lust. I'm emotionally overloaded as it is, can't you see that? I just became a mother, and I'm trying to run a business." Tears filled her eyes. "Oh, damn, now I'm going to cry. Go away, Preston, please. I can't deal with you, with this. I just can't handle anything more. I don't have anywhere to put it."

Preston opened his mouth to speak, then snapped

it closed. Dragging one hand through his hair, he stared at the ceiling for a long moment, then looked at Dinah again.

"Okay, I'll go," he said quietly. "For now. I really don't have anywhere to put this either, Dinah, because I have my own life mapped out. The thing is, I don't like unanswered questions."

"Preston, please." Two tears slid down her pale cheeks.

He took a step toward her. "Don't cry. I'm leaving. Get some sleep, Dinah." He lifted one hand to her face, then hesitated. "Good night." He turned, strode across the room, and left the apartment.

Two more tears flowed down Dinah's cheeks. "Good-bye, Preston," she whispered.

Three

"As you can see, Mr. Harper . . . excuse me, Mr. Hampton," Dinah said, "the contract now reflects all the changes we discussed. The areas of concern to you, as well as those I felt needed attention, now read as they should."

"Excellent," the portly man said. "I'm very impressed with what you've accomplished on my behalf, Miss Bradshaw. All there is left to do is for me to sign it." He wrote his name on the paper with a flourish. "Done."

"And these two other copies need your signature," Dinah said.

The task completed, the man leaned back in his chair and smiled. "That's a tremendous load off my mind. You can be assured that all future contracts I need negotiated will be handled by you."

"Thank you, Mr. Harp—Hampton."

Darn that Preston Harper, Dinah thought. This was Wednesday. She hadn't seen, or spoken to him, since the episode in her apartment the previous Friday night, yet it might as well have been five minutes ago. Preston refused to vacate her mind. His image haunted her during the day, and at night her dreams were filled with vivid, sensual embraces with him. She relieved those incredible kisses over and over, her cheeks often flushing at the memories. Just darn the man.

"I must say, Miss Bradshaw," Mr. Hampton said, bringing Dinah from her disturbing reverie, "your secretary's baby sounds very distressed. She's been crying ever since I arrived."

"Oh, Jenny isn't Anne's baby, she's mine. I'm sorry if her crying annoyed you. Bringing her to the office is a temporary measure that I've taken steps to correct very soon."

"No, no, she isn't annoying me at all," he said. "I raised six of my own, and I'm the proud grandfather of eight. I just hate to hear a baby cry so hard for so long. I'm a soft touch when it comes to the little ones. Why don't you tell your secretary to bring Jenny in here so the sweet thing can see her mama? I have to be on my way in a moment, but let's get that tiny miss smiling again."

"You're very kind." Dinah lifted the telephone

receiver and buzzed her secretary. "Anne? Would you bring Jenny in here now, please?"

"Oh, thank heavens," Anne said. "Her heart is breaking, I swear it is. I can't do a thing to comfort her."

A few moments later the door opened and Anne entered, carrying a wailing Jenny. The baby's face was red and streaked with tears.

"Oh, Jenny," Dinah said, getting to her feet and taking the baby from Anne. "Jenny sweetheart, why are we so unhappy?" She paced the floor, jiggling the screaming infant. "We are so upset, aren't we? What is it, precious? I've checked the book, and I've covered hungry, wet, tired. Jenny, Jenny, hush now."

Mr. Hampton placed his copy of the contract in his briefcase and stood up. "Earache," he said.

Dinah stopped abruptly and stared at him. "What?"

"See how she's tugging on her ear? She doesn't feel well, Miss Bradshaw, and I'd bet you dollars-to-doughnuts that she has an earache. Lord knows my gang had their share of ear infections over the years. I'd suggest you take Jenny to her pediatrician. Well, I'm off. Thanks again for a fine job on this contract. Good-bye."

"Good-bye," Dinah said absently, then snatched her reference book out of the diaper bag. Bouncing Jenny in one arm, she plunked the book on her desk, opened it, and ran her finger down the index.

"Ears, ears," she mumbled. "I never thought of ears. Oh, Jenny, I didn't understand that your pulling on your ear meant—ears. Here it is." She scanned the page she turned to, then placed her hand on Jenny's forehead. "Too warm. Probably a fever. And it says here that a baby will more often than not tug on his ear when . . . oh, I'm so very sorry, sweetheart. Don't cry, please. I'll call Preston right now. Oh, Jenny, forgive me for being such a terrible mother."

Preston walked slowly down the hall of his clinic, frowning at the folder in his hand. He stopped beside Patty's desk.

"Here are Jenny's records," he said. "I've tried to contact her doctor in Chicago, but he's on vacation."

"Why did you call him?" Patty asked.

Preston ran a hand over the back of his neck. "It really wasn't necessary, I suppose. The records are clear and well documented. It's just that Jenny's had a lot of ear infections, and I wanted the Chicago man's opinion as to why."

"Babies are pros at getting ear infections."

"I know but . . ."

"But Jenny is a special Munchkin, right? Do you realize how many times you've mentioned her and Dinah this week? And the week is only half over. Dinah and Jenny are becoming household words around here."

"They are not," Preston said. "I haven't talked about—" He paused. "I have?"

"Yep," Patty said, then she grunted and placed her hands on her protruding stomach. "This baby is kicking the bejeebers out of me today. Up, down, and all around. My back is killing me. Tell me to shut up, Preston. No one wants to hear the complaints of a very pregnant mother-to-be."

"*I* do," he said. "You're unusually uncomfortable, considering you're not due for three more weeks."

"Don't remind me. I'll be black and blue from the inside out at this rate."

"Henry, you should be home with your feet up. We have the temporary receptionist ready to come in whenever we call her."

"Nope. I'd go crazy sitting around staring at my fat stomach. Billy is having a fit too. The daddy-to-be says I should be home in bed, drinking milk. Men are crazy when it comes to babies. Billy is a big, tough cop, but this tiny creature inside me has him terrified. Ohhh, my aching back."

Preston leaned over her desk and peered at Patty's stomach. "Lighten up in there, kid. You're beating on a very classy lady here."

"Oh, shoo," Patty said, flapping her hands at him. "Go think about beautiful Dinah."

He straightened. "I do *not* think about beautiful Dinah." Only twenty-four hours a day, he added silently. "Pregnancy has affected your brain, madam."

"Ha!" The telephone rang, and Patty picked it up. "Dr. Harper's office . . . Yes . . . Oh, hello, Miss Bradshaw."

Preston stiffened. "Dinah?" he whispered. "She's calling? Why? Is something wrong with Jenny?"

Patty glared at him. "I see," she said into the receiver. "Yes, it's nearly closing time, but we'll wait for you. Bring Jenny right over. . . . You're very welcome. Good-bye." She hung up.

"Well?" Preston said. "Well? What's wrong with Jenny?"

"Would you quit yelling?"

"I'm not yelling!" he yelled. "Dammit, Patty, talk to me."

"Dinah thinks Jenny has an earache."

He snatched the folder off her desk. "Another one? Damn." He looked at Patty again. "Call the service and tell them we're shutting down this phone for the night, then go home."

"Preston, Mary left half an hour ago for a dentist appointment, remember? I don't mind staying and assisting you with Jenny."

"Billy has three inches and thirty pounds on me. If you think I'm getting the clone of Spenser's Hawk mad at me for working you overtime, you're crazy."

Patty laughed. "Okay, okay, I'm out of here."

A few minutes later Patty headed for the door, one hand pressed to the small of her back.

"Put your feet up when you get home, Clyde," Preston called after her.

She waved and left. Preston leaned against the wall and crossed his arms over his chest, Jenny's file still in one hand.

Come on, Dinah, he mentally urged, get here. She was going to end up smack-dab in the middle of rush-hour traffic. Jenny was probably crying, which would upset Dinah. She wouldn't pay proper attention to her driving and— Whoa, Harper. It wasn't like him to be an alarmist. He was always calm under stress and strain.

Right, he thought dryly. Except when it came to Dinah. No woman had ever continually occupied his brain during the day. But Dinah did. No woman had ever plagued his dreams at night, disrupting his sleep. But Dinah did. The simple memory of any other woman's kisses had never caused hot desire to pulse through his body. But Dinah's did.

What was it about her? he wondered. He'd left her apartment last Friday night with unanswered questions he'd later decided were best left alone. So why in hell was Dinah Bradshaw mentally following him around twenty-four hours a day? That woman was driving him straight out of his tree.

"Driving," he muttered. Dinah was in rush-hour

traffic with a screaming baby and— "Harper, for Pete's sake, shut up."

The door suddenly opened and Dinah rushed in. A whimpering Jenny was clinging to her neck.

"Oh, Preston," she said in a trembling voice.

He was moving before he realized it, crossing the room and pulling both Dinah and Jenny into his arms. He inhaled the aromas of lilac cologne and baby powder, and filled his being with the feel of the woman and baby.

Dinah was there. And Jenny was there. Where they belonged. Safe and protected with him. Nothing was going to happen to harm either one of them. *Nothing.*

"Dada," Jenny said with a sob.

He released his hold on them. "I'm here, Munchkin," he said, lifting her into his arms. "Let's go have a look at you." He turned and started toward the examining room with Dinah right behind him. "I'm going to fix you up, Jenny babe."

"Oh, Preston," Dinah said, "it's all my fault. I didn't understand what it meant, the way she was pulling on her ear. She was crying for so long and . . . I read the book but . . . It took a client of mine two seconds to recognize what was wrong with her. I'm a miserable excuse for a mother. I didn't know she was in pain and—"

Preston stopped so suddenly, Dinah bumped into him. He turned and frowned at her.

"You hold it right there," he said. "No one but

you expects you to be an instant authority on raising a baby. If it were that easy, then why the hell did I spend all those years in medical school finding out what makes these little people tick? Quit being so hard on yourself, quit feeling sorry for yourself, and let's concentrate on Jenny." He pivoted again and strode into the first examining room.

Dinah blinked, then hurried after him.

Preston tossed Jenny's file onto the examining table, then sat the baby down. She cried, raising her arms to him, and he began talking to her, telling her about his buddy, Robert Rabbit, who wore red, high-top tennis shoes and a green tuxedo wherever he went. Jenny hiccuped, stuck her thumb in her mouth, and riveted her teary gaze on Preston while he inspected her ears.

Dinah sank onto a stool and set the diaper bag on the floor. Closing her eyes, she allowed Preston's soothing voice to flow over her in a comforting wave.

Dear Lord, she was exhausted, she thought. She was physically and emotionally drained. When she'd relinquished Jenny into Preston's care, it was as though she'd placed her own well-being in his hands as well.

She was granting herself the luxury of leaning on him, trusting in his knowledge as a doctor . . . and his strength and kindness as a man. And it felt wonderful.

Preston had been right the other night when he said something special was happening between them. Yet as tempted as she was to follow the urges of her heart and body, she knew this was not the time in her life for a man like Preston Harper. He wasn't hers to have . . . not now.

"Okay, Munchkin," he said, and Dinah opened her eyes. "You were a super girl. I wouldn't want some big lug poking around in *my* ears, by golly. You're a real trooper, Jenny."

"Hello, hello," a voice called from the outer office.

"In here, Mother," Preston answered. "Lock the front door, would you, please?"

A minute later Elizabeth Harper appeared in the open doorway to the examining room.

"Mother," Preston said, "this is Dinah Bradshaw, and this crabby Munchkin is Jenny. Dinah, my mother, Elizabeth Harper."

Dinah got to her feet. "Hello, Mrs. Harper."

"Oh, call me Elizabeth, dear, as does the world."

"What's doin', Ma?" Preston asked. "Are you out on the streets, into the bars?"

"That was the plan," Elizabeth said. "But when I saw that your car was still here, I decided to see if you'd like the honor of buying me dinner before you make your hospital rounds."

"My mother's a mooch," Preston said to Dinah. "It's a sad fact I try to hide from the general populace."

"Ignore him, Dinah," Elizabeth said. "What a beautiful baby. Not a happy one, but very pretty."

"Thank you," Dinah said, and turned to Preston. "How's Jenny?"

"Not bad. She has a slight ear infection, but we caught it early, thanks to her loud announcement of its existence."

"Which I didn't understand," Dinah said, shaking her head.

"Don't start that again," he warned her. "I mean it, Dinah. You're doing fine with Jenny, just fine. Hey, my mother had her paws on me from day one, didn't know diddly about babies, and I survived. You just got Jenny, remember? You're a brand new single parent, and this isn't an easy ball game you jumped into the middle of, but you're *not* striking out at the plate. Trust me a bit here, okay? You're a good mother, Dinah."

"Thank you, Preston," she whispered. "You're . . . I . . ." She shook her head, unable to speak further.

Their gazes met, and time stopped.

"We need a plan," Elizabeth said after a minute. The sound of her voice startled both Dinah and Preston back to reality. "Ear infections call for antibiotics, which means a trip to the pharmacy. Dinah dear, you're exhausted, and so is Jenny. Therefore, I'll go for the prescription while you take Jenny home. Preston, make your rounds at the hospital, then bring a super-supreme pizza loaded with everything to Dinah's so we can all eat. I'll need Dinah's address. Everyone have their assignments? Let's get moving. We have a Munchkin here who'd like to feel better."

"But—but you don't even know me," Dinah said.

Elizabeth smiled. "Oh, I think I do, dear. Yes, I believe I know you very well, and it is, indeed, a pleasure to meet you."

"Mother, you're in your fruitcake mode," Preston said, "but I'll go so far as to say your plan has merit. You're into making much sense otherwise, but we'll chalk that up to your age. I can only pray it isn't hereditary." He turned to Dinah and picked up the file. "According to the records I received from Chicago, Jenny has a history of frequent ear infections."

Dinah's eyes widened. "Really? What does that mean?"

He shrugged. "Probably nothing more than that she's prone to ear infections. Another baby just as healthy as Jenny might catch a cold at every turn. I was going to ask the Chicago doctor's opinion, but he's on vacation. I'd say that since we're aware of it now, we'll simply be on the lookout for any signs of ear problems, and nip them in the bud."

"Fine," Elizabeth said. "Enough chatter. It's time to leap into action."

Preston chuckled. "Yes, Colonel Harper. Is all this okay with you, Dinah?"

"Oh, yes. I can't tell you how grateful I am for—"

"Later, dear," Elizabeth said. "Preston, write out the prescription for Jenny. Oh, and don't forget the extra cheese on the pizza."

"Ah," Jenny said.

The three adults laughed, and Dinah felt a lovely warmth sweep through her, calming her frazzled nerves.

This, she thought, was what it was like to be part of a caring family. It had been so long since she'd belonged to anyone. She'd never dwelled on her aloneness, but had simply accepted it. Since she'd met Preston, though . . . No, she had to keep her thoughts, and herself, under her command.

Elizabeth hustled her and Jenny out the door, and as Dinah drove home, Preston's parting words—*I'll be there soon*—replayed over and over in her mind.

Two hours later Preston rode up in the elevator in Dinah's building, a large, flat box of pizza in his hands.

He was eager to get there, he realized. He'd even driven above the speed limit from the hospital. Never before had he gotten so charged up over sharing a pizza with a woman. He was definitely losing it.

His strategy of simply dismissing the unanswered questions about what was happening between them hadn't worked at all. So it was time for a new plan. He *had* to get Dinah out of his system so he could focus on his patients and his goal of adopting a baby.

Staying away from Dinah only heightened her appeal, he mused. Therefore, he'd switch tactics and see her as much as possible. Soon he'd realize she was simply an attractive, intelligent woman, not some strange being who could weave an eerie spell over his mind and body.

Great idea, and it would do the trick.

Wouldn't it?

"It sure as hell better," he mumbled as he stepped out of the elevator.

A smiling Dinah opened the door for him. He ignored the increased tempo of his heart as his gaze skimmed over her enticing figure clad in jeans and a pale yellow sweatshirt. He said hello to the air above her head, avoiding looking into her eyes.

"Pizza delivery," he said, stepping into the apartment.

She shut the door. "It smells heavenly."

"And we're starving," Elizabeth added. "Bring it over here to the table, Preston. The drinks are poured, and we're all set to go."

He crossed the room to the small dining alcove. "How's Jenny?"

"Asleep," Elizabeth said. "We gave her liquid Tylenol and the antibiotic, per your instructions,

Doctor. She ate, and went to bed without a squeak of protest. The little darling is all worn out."

The three sat down at the table and in unison reached for slices of pizza. They ate in silence until they'd taken the edge off their appetites.

"Dinah and I had a lovely chat," Elizabeth said finally. "She told me how she came to have Jenny."

"Mmm," Preston said, his mouth full of pizza.

"Dinah said you told her about your plans to adopt a baby," Elizabeth went on. "Have you heard anything from the social services?"

Preston took a sip of his soft drink. "No, but Jack said they have a heavy caseload. He'll do everything he can to get them moving. I've called a lot of doctors I know, so the word is out about my wanting a baby. All I can do is be patient and wait." He turned to Dinah. "Did you take Jenny's temperature?"

"No," she said. "Was I supposed to?"

"No, not really. She was a little warm, but nothing to get excited about. The liquid Tylenol should have taken care of it." He stood up. "I'll go check on her, though."

"Your pizza will get cold, dear," Elizabeth said pleasantly.

"I won't be long."

He strode across the room, and Elizabeth laughed softly. Dinah looked at her questioningly.

"Oh, pay no attention to me, Dinah," Elizabeth

said. "I'm just having a marvelous time, that's all."

Dinah stared at Elizabeth for a long moment, then shrugged and reached for another slice of pizza.

After satisfying himself that Jenny was cool and sleeping peacefully, Preston stood by the crib gazing down at her.

Images of Dinah floated in his mental vision, and the now-familiar heat coiled low in his body. He was sharing a pizza with Dinah at the end of a long day, he mused. A not very good pizza, at that, yet there was something special about the event, a sense of . . . coming home.

He rubbed one hand over his face. He was no longer losing it, he thought. He'd completely lost it. His decision to become a single father had not been made quickly. He'd analyzed his situation for months, until he'd reached the conclusion that he couldn't have it all without something, someone, suffering from neglect.

But ever since he'd met Dinah Bradshaw everything had changed. His course of action, his goals, had been crystal-clear, yet now . . .

Preston stiffened. Was it possible? he wondered. Was he falling in love with Dinah?

No!

But there was so much about Dinah to love.

The independent side of her that let him know she was her own woman and would never cling to a man; and the softer side, that allowed her to lean on him when she needed to. She was intelligent, warm, beautiful, courageous. A devoted mother, a successful attorney . . . The list went on and on.

But there was a glitch, as there'd always been in the past. Dinah was perfect for him . . . almost. The one missing piece to the picture made the remainder fall apart. Dinah was dedicated to her career. She had set goals she intended to achieve, with no stopping along the way to fall in love and marry.

Yes, she had Jenny, and she was doing a helluva fine job with her. But she had adamantly made it clear that she had no room in her life now for a man. For him.

He couldn't have it all.

He couldn't have Dinah Bradshaw.

Ignoring the hollow ache within him at that thought, Preston left the bedroom and started back down the hall. The sound of Dinah's laughter reached him, and he stopped, closing his eyes for a moment. The lilting resonance seemed to wrap around him, making it difficult for him to breathe.

No, he reaffirmed in his mind. He would not fall in love with Dinah.

He sat back down at the table, glanced at the

remaining pizza, and decided he'd had enough to eat.

"Jenny is fine," he said. "She's snoring."

"I'm going to baby-sit her tomorrow," Elizabeth said. "I don't have a thing on my calendar, and she can stay quiet, beat that nasty ear infection before it worsens."

He looked at his mother, puzzled by her offer. "That's very nice of you."

"My feelings exactly," Dinah said. "I've come to the conclusion that you Harpers are very special people. I'm extremely fortunate to have found such wonderful friends."

Your wife is your best friend, Preston thought. So you're your wife's best friend and—

A beeping noise interrupted his thoughts. He pressed a button on the small black box clipped to his belt and stood up.

"My service," he said. "May I use your phone, Dinah?"

"Yes, of course."

After talking for a few minutes, he hung up the phone and turned to them. "I have to go. Patty is in labor at the hospital."

"She isn't due yet," Elizabeth said.

"Her baby has other ideas. I promised her I'd be the attending pediatrician when the baby was born."

"Call me at home and fill me in," Elizabeth said. "I don't care what time it is. Patty and Billy are like part of the family. I'll want to know the baby has safely arrived and Patty is fine."

"Okay." Preston started toward the door, then stopped and glanced at Dinah. "This is how it is, you know. Not a minute's peace. I didn't even finish my pizza. I can't remember when I've seen the end of a movie, Dinah, or heard an entire concert. The old beeper goes off and I've got to go. Munchkins are demanding little buggers, and when they need me, they need me. Can't postpone them, not for a second. So, this is how my life is, all the time. Grim, huh? Well, see you."

He slammed the door behind him, leaving Dinah gaping.

"What on earth came over him?" she asked his mother. "I've never heard him blither like that."

Elizabeth Harper just smiled.

At three A.M. Preston stood next to Billy outside the nursery window at the hospital.

"You have a fine son, Billy," he said quietly. "He's healthy as a horse, and a good size, especially considering he made his entrance into the world early. Patty is doing great too."

"I can't believe this," Billy said. "God, Preston, look at him. He's something, isn't he? I'm a father. I . . . am . . . a . . . father. Holy smokes, what a terrifying thought. No, no, it's super." he laughed. "Lord, I'm a wreck."

Preston patted Billy on the shoulder. "Go home and get some sleep. You can see Patty tomorrow. . . . Well, it's already tomorrow, but you know what I mean. I'm going to hit the sack myself."

Billy pumped Preston's hand vigorously. "Thanks for everything. I know it meant a lot to Patty to have you here. It made it easier for me to wait, too, because you were on the scene." He shook his head. "Dear Lord, Preston, I have a son. I have a beautiful wife, a fantastic baby. A family. I'm the luckiest man alive."

Preston smiled. "You sure are. I'll talk to you later."

Leaving Billy still gazing rapturously at his son, Preston walked slowly down the silent hallway. Fatigue settled over him like an oppressive weight. Billy's parting words bounced around in his mind the whole way home. Wife . . . baby . . . family . . . family . . . family . . .

When Preston entered his big, dark house, the silence seemed to beat against his weary body.

He stood motionless, frozen by the most chilling sense of loneliness he'd ever known.

Four

Preston rotated his neck back and forth in an attempt to loosen the aching muscles, then redirected his attention to the file on his desk. After writing several more lines of data regarding the patient, he tossed the pen onto the desk.

He was getting too old for sleepless nights like the one he'd just endured, he thought, yawning. Then he frowned. Actually, he'd had the opportunity to sleep for several hours after Patty's baby had been born.

Once again, though, Dinah Bradshaw had followed him into bed. He hadn't slept a wink. She was a very annoying woman, and he'd had enough of this garbage.

Lord, he was in a lousy mood, he thought. He

was tired and irritable, and blaming Dinah for his own lack of self-control.

"Take command of yourself, Harper," he muttered.

"Excuse me, Dr. Harper?"

He looked up. Patty's replacement, an attractive young woman, stood in his office doorway.

"Come in, Judy," he said. "Is everything okay up front?"

"Yes. You've seen your last scheduled patient for today. According to the list of instructions Patty left me, we'll stay open for another hour to handle any emergencies. Here's your mail." She crossed the room and handed him the stack of envelopes.

"Thanks. Listen, you and Mary take off. I'll handle the phone for the next hour."

"Are you sure?"

"Yep, no problem. You did fine today, Judy. This place can turn into a zoo, and you were cool under fire."

"I enjoyed it, except when three kids were screaming at once." She smiled. "I never realized they could be that loud. Well, good night. I'll tell Mary we can leave, and I'll see you tomorrow."

"Fine. Good night."

Silence fell over the room as Preston sorted through his mail, tossing more envelopes in the wastebasket than he kept on his desk. He opened a large manila one and pulled out what was at least a dozen sheets of paper. He scanned the cover letter, then flipped through the other pages.

"Brother," he said aloud.

Social services had leapt into action but good. They apparently wanted to know everything about him from the day he was born. He'd better get started on the paperwork right away. It was an important step toward his goal of having at long last his own child.

The image of Jenny suddenly superimposed itself over the letter he was staring at. He blinked and shook his head, but a smiling Jenny remained firmly in place.

The telephone rang and he reached for it quickly, relieved to be diverted from the strange tricks his tired mind was playing on him.

"Dr. Harper," he said into the receiver.

"Hello, dear."

"Mother! Why are you calling? Is Jenny all right?"

"Preston, Jenny is fine, which I've told you each of the seven times you phoned me today to check on her."

"I didn't call you seven times. Five . . . maybe. Or six."

"Seven."

"Well, so what?"

"I see your sunshine mood didn't improve during the day."

"I was up all night, Mother. Did you phone for

the sadistic pleasure of harassing me, or is there something on your mind?"

"Preston, go to your room and take a nap until you're a human being again."

He chuckled. "Point taken. I'm behaving like a rotten little kid. I humbly apologize, Mrs. Harper. How may I be of service to you, ma'am?"

"That's much better. Now then, I've just spoken with Clancy. We've been assigned to the craft booth for the annual bazaar at the hospital. She has a stack of craft books we can go through for ideas, so I suggested she come here to Dinah's this evening. She and I can pore over the books, and Jenny will have a chance to get to know Clancy better."

"I see."

"Marvelous idea, isn't it? You lucky boy, you have a genius for a mother."

"I'll pass on that one."

"Anyway, the second half of the plan is for you to take Dinah out to dinner. That poor girl could use a break, Preston. She's been under tremendous stress, and a quiet meal in a cozy restaurant would do her a world of good."

Ah-ha. This was perfect, Preston thought, his mind racing. His new strategy for breaking Dinah's spell over him was to be with her as much as possible.

"Excellent," he said. "I'll call her right now. If

you don't hear from me, assume it was agreeable with her."

"It's up to you to convince her to go to dinner. She'll probably feel she should rush home to Jenny. I'm not interfering in your social life, Preston. This is all from a medical standpoint, you understand. Dinah needs an evening away from the sudden, unexpected pressures she's been dealing with."

"Yes, of course. This is all in the line of medical duty. No problem."

"And Jenny can get to know Clancy."

"Right."

"Well, have a lovely dinner. Good-bye for now, dear."

"How's Jenny?"

Elizabeth sighed. "She's fine, fine, fine. Good-bye."

There was a sharp click as Elizabeth hung up with a less-than-gentle touch. Preston glared at the receiver for a moment before returning it to its cradle.

Dinner with Dinah, he mused. Yes, it was an excellent idea. He reached for the phone again.

She was going out to dinner with Preston Harper, Dinah thought incredulously.

Realizing she was still holding the phone, she quickly dropped it into place.

Preston had rattled off his invitation, along with the rationale of Jenny getting to know Clancy better and Dinah herself getting a break. She'd bobbed her head up and down like a puppet, and there she was . . . less than an hour away from going out to dinner with Preston.

Was this a good idea? she wondered. She was having enough trouble keeping thoughts of him at bay. Should she really see him when she didn't have Jenny to act as a buffer?

She pushed back from her desk and walked into the small bathroom off her office. Her reflection in the mirror revealed a somewhat wan face, her hair pulled into a neat but unflattering bun, and her tailored suit, softened slightly by the bow at the neck of her pale blue blouse.

She looked, she decided, like an attorney. But it wasn't the lawyer who was going out with Preston, nor was it Jenny's mother. It was Dinah, the woman.

But was that a good idea?

Yes, perhaps it was. Without Jenny there, she and Preston would interact on a totally different plane. They could very well discover that they found each other as dull as dishwater, with absolutely nothing in common.

The sensual pull between them would be revealed as nothing more than simple physical attraction, and that would be that. She'd regain control of her wayward thoughts and get herself back on the proper track.

Excellent, she thought.

"Dinah?"

She stepped out of the bathroom. "Yes, Anne?"

"I just wanted to say good night," Anne said. "I hope Jenny is totally recovered from her ear infection."

"Every time I called home today to check, Preston's mother said she was doing just fine. In fact, I've agreed to go out to dinner with Preston so that Jenny can get to know Clancy better. Clancy is going to my apartment to spend the evening with Jenny and Mrs. Harper . . . Elizabeth. She did tell me to call her Elizabeth."

"Ah," Anne said. "The grandma types baby-sit while the dad and mom types go out to dine. Why, I do declare, Ms. Bradshaw, y'all are just one big happy family."

Dinah laughed. "Would you stop? Preston and I aren't going out to dinner." She paused. "Well, we are, but it's not a *date*, because . . . why am I explaining all this to you?"

"Beats me. I get the feeling you're trying to explain it to yourself."

"Oh, well, I—" Dinah threw up her hands. "Never mind. I'll see you tomorrow."

"Have a lovely time," Anne said as she left the room.

Dinah glared at the doorway for a moment, then

dashed back into the bathroom and began to pull the pins from her hair. She brushed it vigorously, until it was a shiny tumble of waves. After spraying her lilac-scented cologne across her throat and freshening her makeup, she again peered at her reflection.

So-so, she thought. Sort of halfway between the lawyer and the woman.

She slipped off her suit jacket, then pulled the bow from around her neck. She tied it as a sash around her waist, allowing the silky strands to trail along one thigh. After opening the top button on her blouse, she freed the second . . . then the third, smoothing the material to reveal a glimpse of the lacy top of her slip.

"Well now," she said, wiggling her eyebrows at her reflection. "I am woman. W-o-m-a-n."

She left the bathroom with an exaggerated sway to her hips and what she decided was a sultry, sexy expression on her face.

Then she stopped so suddenly, she teetered on her high heels. Her eyes widened and her mouth dropped open.

Preston Harper was standing in her office, wearing black slacks, a steel-gray shirt with a gray paisley tie, and a gray sport coat.

His hair somehow seemed thicker, darker, his face more handsome than the last time she'd seen him. He was gazing directly at her, his eyes pinning her in place, as if she were a trapped butterfly.

"Hello, Dinah," he said quietly.

"Hello, Preston." Her voice sounded strangely breathless.

Neither spoke further, nor moved. They stared at each other as their hearts raced and desire swelled within them.

Oh, dear Lord, Dinah thought, she was so glad to see him. She wanted to run across the room and fling herself into his arms. She wanted him to hug her and kiss her. Oh, yes, she definitely felt like a woman, and Preston was the most incredible man she'd ever met.

"Shall we go?" he asked.

"What? Oh, yes, of course. I'll just get my purse. Maybe I should call and check on Jenny first."

He laughed. "Not if you value your life. I've already driven my mother crazy with my calls."

"You've been phoning about Jenny too?"

He nodded. "She's a very special Munchkin, Dinah."

"Yes. Yes, she is. Well . . . um, off we go."

Preston's gaze remained riveted to Dinah as she retrieved her purse and jacket from the bathroom, flicked on her answering machine, and turned out the lights.

He watched every move she made as she locked the office and walked beside him to his sports car.

He scrutinized her as she slid onto the bucket

seat, smoothed her skirt over her knees, and smiled up at him as he closed the door.

And he knew.

As he slowly walked around the back of the car, he struggled to come to grips with the indisputable truth.

He was in love with Dinah Bradshaw.

How in the blue blazes had this happened to him? he wondered in a sudden panic. After all these years, just when he had his life figured out, his goals clearly defined, Dinah happened.

He got into the car and yanked the door closed. His jaw set in a hard line, he revved the engine and peeled out of the parking lot.

His head began to throb in rhythm with the messages hammering against his mind.

He couldn't be in love with Dinah Bradshaw.

He couldn't have it all.

What was he going to do?

"Preston?" Dinah asked. "Is something wrong?"

Everything was wrong, dammit. "No. No, I'm fine. I was just thinking about something." He managed to smile briefly at her. "There are a lot of out-of-state licenses. The snow birds are arriving."

"Well, it's nearly October. It's getting chilly up north."

"You must be glad you're not there anymore." His entire life was coming apart at the seams, and he was talking about the weather? Lord above, he was losing his mind. "Florida is the place to be in the winter. Sunshine and oranges."

"Next summer I'll take Jenny to the beach. I'll have to be careful about how much sun she gets, though. The book is very firm about not exposing a child to a great deal of direct sunlight. I'll get her a pail and shovel and—no."

"No? Your book doesn't allow pails and shovels?"

"That's not what I meant. The no is for, no, I'm not going to talk about Jenny tonight. I'm neither a lawyer nor a mother this evening. I'm just Dinah Bradshaw."

And he was in love with her, Preston thought dismally.

The expensive restaurant had a cozy and romantic atmosphere. A combo played dreamy music on the far side of a gleaming dance floor. The food was delicious, the service efficient.

Everything was perfect, Dinah thought, except for the fact that with every beat of her heart, she became increasingly aware that Preston was not as dull as dishwater. They even had endless things in common. Each time they laughed together or their eyes met, delicate, heart-warming emotions intertwined with the now-familiar desire swirling within her.

She was, she decided, in a heap of trouble. Her attraction for Preston kept growing stronger. She had the ridiculous urge to cheer as they not only agreed on favorite books and movies, but on the values by which they shaped their lives.

They were so right together.

And it was all so wrong.

She was becoming a befuddled mess, Dinah thought. Her mind knew there was no hope for a future with Preston. Maybe there would have been if they had met several years down the road, but not now. Their plans and paths were set on opposite courses.

But her heart? Her heart was whispering messages of love. Was she falling in love with Preston?

"Dinah?" he said.

"No." She blinked. "Oh, I'm sorry. I was miles away. Did you ask me something?"

"Would you like to dance?"

She smiled. "I'd be delighted."

He stood up, then assisted her from her chair. She gave him another dazzling smile and allowed him to guide her to the dance floor.

This, she thought, was one of the dumbest things she'd ever done. Sitting across the table from the man with candlelight flickering over his gorgeous face had already thrown her into a tizzy.

Now, like a complete dolt, she was going to let herself be nestled close to his magnificent body while they swayed to romantic music. She would feel his strength and warmth, and relive once again the kisses they'd shared.

Yes, this was really dumb. And she wished those people would get out of the way so she and Preston could get to the dance floor faster.

Preston took her into his arms and began to dance to the delicate strains of a waltz. He inhaled deeply, intoxicated by the scent of her sweet perfume, and pulled her closer.

He was out of his mind, of course, he realized calmly. He was in love with a woman he didn't *want* to be in love with, and he should be heading for the hills at top speed.

But not him, he thought dryly. He was adding fuel to the fire already burning within him, and that fire was about to explode out of control.

He loved Dinah Bradshaw. And he wanted Dinah Bradshaw.

The future, he mused, was a mess. Hell, the present was a disaster. But right now, with Dinah in his arms, fitting against him as though made just for him, he didn't care.

He tightened his hold on her even more.

The waltz ended and another began.

Dinah blanked her mind and filled her senses with Preston. She refused to think. She simply savored the sensations rushing through her, and the essence of the man holding her so securely in his strong arms. Her breasts were crushed to his chest with a sweet pain.

He smelled like woodsy after-shave, soap, and man. She could feel the power in his thighs as he moved her across the floor and—oh, glorious heaven—his arousal, pressing against her.

"Dinah?" he said quietly. "Can you feel what you're doing to me?"

"Yes," she whispered.

"I think we'd better end this evening right now. I'll take you back to your office, then I'll follow you home so I'll know you got there safely."

The voices of Dinah's logical mind warred with those of her heart, creating a cacophony that echoed in her head.

This was *her* night, she thought. She was Dinah Bradshaw, woman. Nothing more and most definitely nothing less. Reality was beyond the safe circle of Preston's embrace, a hazy blur that held no great importance in these stolen hours.

That she might be falling in love with Preston didn't matter, not now. That she was inching toward potential heartache didn't matter. That she might regret the price she'd pay for what she did that night didn't matter.

"Yes, Preston," she said softly, "please follow me home."

As though surrounded by a misty, sensual fog, Dinah was only vaguely aware of leaving the restaurant, returning to her office, then driving to her apartment with Preston's headlights reflected in her rearview mirror.

She supposed that she said the proper thank-yous and good nights to Elizabeth and Clancy.

Then the two women were gone, and she turned to look at Preston.

He was standing by the bookcase, and she could feel the sexual tension crackling through the air.

"Dinah . . ." He stopped to clear his throat. "I'd better go. I want to make love to you so badly that I ache." *Because I love you,* he added silently. "But consenting adults or not, I don't think it would be a good idea because . . . because it . . . just wouldn't be . . . a good idea." He raked a hand through his hair. "Hell."

Listen to him, Dinah's mind yelled, *He's right.*

But this was Preston, her heart countered. This was the man who evoked desire within her like none before. This was the first man, the only man, who had ever caused her to wonder if she was falling in love. It was the wrong place and time, but she knew Preston was the right man.

"Preston, I—"

"You know what I'm saying is true, Dinah," he went on, talking too fast. "You're a very organized, orderly person. I mean, Lord, you even raise Jenny with one eye on a reference book. You and I have so much going for us. . . . But actually, we don't, because our individual plans for the future are set and—Dammit!" he suddenly yelled. "Would you tell me to get the hell out of here?"

No, she thought. She wanted him to stay and make love with her. She wanted to hold fast to the tiny ember of hope glowing within her that she and Preston *could* have a future together, nurture that hope until it became a brightly burning flame of truth.

But it *wasn't* true, she admitted to herself. Preston wanted a baby but not a wife. He desired her, but he wouldn't make room for her in his life. Even if she somehow juggled her own timetable regarding her career plans, it would make no difference to Preston and the road he had chosen for himself.

She had to ignore the ember of hope within her, until it died of neglect.

"You're right, Preston," she said, her voice unsteady. "It would be best if you left now."

He stared up at the ceiling for a long moment, then looked at her again. "No."

She frowned. "What?"

He closed the distance between them and framed her face with his hands. He stared directly at her, and she held his gaze.

"I'll leave," he said, his voice raspy, "but I suddenly don't like my asking you to chase me out of here because I'm afraid if I touch you, I'll lose control. I'm a man, not a randy boy. Even more, I respect you, admire you . . ." Love you. "Care about you. I need to know that we're agreeing, together, that this just isn't the time for us to make love."

Never before, Dinah thought, had she felt so cherished, so special. She didn't dare, at that moment, try to figure out if she was in love with

Preston, because knowing would serve no purpose. She would simply tuck away in her heart the precious gift he had just given her.

"Thank you," she said softly. "I . . . thank you."

He lowered his head and brushed his lips over hers. She shivered at the fleeting caress, and he dropped his hands from her face to put his arms around her. Claiming her mouth in a searing kiss, he parted her lips, seeking her tongue, molding her body to his.

Then slowly, reluctantly, he ended the kiss and stepped back, releasing his hold on her and forcing her to drop her arms from around his neck.

Their eyes met, sending messages of warmth and desire . . . and of a deep understanding and trust that seemed to touch their very souls.

"Preston," Dinah finally said, breaking the magical spell, "I have some wickedly expensive brandy that my friend Sylvia gave me for Christmas last year. Would you care for a nightcap before you go?"

He smiled. "I'd be delighted."

"Make yourself comfortable. I'm going to look in on Jenny, then I'll get the brandy."

A short time later they were seated on the sofa, a few safe inches separating them as they sipped the liquor.

"Your friend, Sylvia," Preston said, "has excellent taste in brandy."

"I hadn't even opened it until now," Dinah said.

"It certainly warms a person right down to their toes."

"True. I think if anyone drank more than an inch or so at a time, they'd pass out on their face." He took another sip and nodded. "Excellent. And a perfect way to end a lovely evening."

"Yes, I—oh!" she shrieked.

Water! Icy cold water suddenly sprayed down on them from the ceiling with the force of a waterfall.

"Good Lord!" Preston exclaimed. He lunged to his feet, pulling her up with him. "Something has set off the sprinkler system in here."

The sound of Jenny wailing rose above the spraying water.

"And in Jenny's room," he said, swiping water out of his eyes. "Probably the whole apartment. We've got to get out. I'll go for Jenny."

"Ohmigod, ohmigod," Dinah said, her eyes wide as the water beat against her. "Ohmigod."

He returned with a screaming Jenny wrapped in a blanket, and they burst out of the apartment into the hall. Several other tenants were already there, most dressed in pajamas or robes. The hall offered no shelter, though. Water streamed from those sprinklers as well.

"Is there a fire?" someone yelled. "I don't smell smoke."

"We'd better evacuate," a man said. "Use the stairs. Elevators aren't safe in a fire. Stay calm, everyone."

"Calm, hell," a woman replied. "I'm soaked to the skin and freezing to death. Let's get the hell out of here."

The water suddenly stopped, shocking everyone but Jenny into silence. A moment later the stairway door opened, and three firemen in bright yellow slickers stepped into the hall.

"There's no fire, folks," one said. "There was a short in the electrical system on this floor that activated the sprinklers. You're in no danger, except for maybe catching a cold. Everything appears to be pretty soaked, so I'd suggest you find someplace else to stay until the damage can be assessed and everything dried out."

"Life is not dull," Preston said. "Jenny, you're okay, so you can shut off your siren. Come on, Dinah, let's get you and Jenny some dry clothes . . . if there are any."

"But—"

"Don't argue. Jenny's just getting over an ear infection, remember?"

"Ohmigod," she said. "Oh, Dinah, shut up."

They went back into the apartment and Dinah stopped abruptly, horror flooding over her as she stared at the destruction in her living room.

Everything was soaked. Already ugly white patches marked the puddles on the wood furniture. Water beaded on the tops of her stereo equipment and VCR, and dripped off the bookshelves.

She imagined she could see the expensive hard-cover books swelling with moisture.

The overstuffed sofa and chairs were absorbing the pooled water like thirsty beasts quenching their dry throats. The wallpaper was streaked beyond savings, and the matted photographs of the ocean that decorated one wall were ruined.

"Oh" was all Dinah was able to say before her throat closed with unshed tears.

"Hey, easy," Preston said gently. "It looks terrible, but everything will be replaced, or repaired, by the owner of the building. It was an accident. There was no fire, no one was hurt."

"Yes, of course," she said, her voice trembling. "These are material things, that's all. We're safe and sound, the three of us. I'm really very grateful for that. But—"

"I know. This is your home, your haven, and you worked very hard for these possessions. It'll be set to rights, Dinah, you'll see."

She nodded, swallowing past the lump in her throat.

"Let's pack up some clothes for you and Jenny," he went on, "and get the hell out of here. Jenny is chilled, and I don't want her to have a relapse."

Dinah snapped her head around to look at Jenny. She had stopped crying, and was methodically poking Preston's chin with one tiny finger.

"Dear Lord, where is my mind?" she said. "Jenny

is the important one here, not the condition of the furniture and books. Dandy mother I am."

"Don't start that routine," Preston said, walking across the room. "I'll change Jenny and gather up some things for her. You pack enough for tomorrow for yourself, then we can come back for more later."

"All right," Dinah said, following him down the hall. "Jenny and I will check into a hotel and—"

Preston stopped abruptly.

"No way," he said, looking at her over his shoulder. "You're both coming home with me."

Five

A short time later Dinah was driving her car with Jenny strapped in her carrier in the backseat. Dinah was following Preston, and not really paying attention to where they were going. She was too busy dealing with reality.

The magical night, the wondrous, glorious hours as Dinah, the woman, with Preston, the man were over. She had grabbed hold of a fragment of time and savored it, as if it were a delicious red and white striped peppermint stick.

But the magical evening, just like a peppermint stick, had dissolved into nothing, with only lingering memories to prove that it had ever existed.

Dinah sighed. She was exhausted, both physically and mentally. Her mind was filled with confusion, and all she wanted to do was sleep.

She pulled herself back to attention as the blinker on Preston's car flashed, and he turned into a driveway of a large two-story house silhouetted in the bright moonlight.

In a blur of fatigue she was vaguely aware of Preston talking to Jenny in that special, low voice of his as he carried the baby into the house, the diaper bag in his other hand. Dinah followed with her suitcase, forcing one foot in front of the other.

She glanced at the huge living room when Preston turned on the lights, but was too dazed to notice anything except the enormous stone fireplace that covered nearly one entire wall.

She trudged up the stairs behind Preston and into the first bedroom on the right. Setting her suitcase on the floor, she took Jenny from him, then watched as he dragged the mattress off one of the twin beds.

"We'll get a dry mattress for her crib tomorrow," he said. "She can sleep on this on the floor tonight, and we won't have to worry about her falling off the bed. We'll have to leave the door shut, though, so she doesn't crawl out of the room and head for the stairs."

He settled Jenny on the sheet-covered mattress and pulled the blanket over her. Jenny wiggled, stuck her bottom in the air, her thumb in her mouth, and closed her eyes.

"Munchkins go with the flow," he said, smiling. "Okay, I'm going to get out of these wet clothes and take a hot shower. There's actually enough of this night left to get a few hours sleep before we have to be up for work."

No, Dinah thought. There was nothing left of the night, not really. Not the magical night it had been.

"I'll sleep in the other twin bed in here," she said. "I'm so tired, I feel as though I could sleep for a week. I appreciate all you've done, Preston."

"Don't thank me. I want you here. Hell, Dinah, I want you next to me in my bed. I want to wake up in a few hours and make love to you at dawn's light, but . . . enough said. Good night, Dinah. Sleep well."

"Good night, Preston."

He left the room, closing the door behind him, only to open it again a second later.

"This is ridiculous," he said, crossing the room to her. "I'm not going to say good night to you as if I were your brother."

"But . . ."

He pulled her into his arms and brought his mouth down onto hers.

Dinah's eyes widened in shock, then they drifted closed as the kiss gentled. Preston's tongue stroked hers in a maddening, sensual rhythm. She encircled his waist with her arms and pressed against him, wanting, needing, so much more.

He stiffened abruptly, jerking his head up and taking a step back. She swayed unsteadily and opened her eyes.

"I'm sorry," he said, his voice hoarse with passion. "I'm not thinking straight. This has been a rather unsettling evening. Get some sleep. Good night, Dinah." He turned and strode from the room, closing the door behind him with a decisive click.

She stared after him, placing her hand over her heart as if to slow its racing tempo. Then with a weary sigh she turned to open her suitcase.

Preston stood under the hot water in the shower, feeling the chill ebb from his body.

He had never been so confused in his life. He loved Dinah, and to make her his wife and darling, adorable Jenny his daughter would be heaven. They would be a family—Preston, Dinah, Jenny, and any children he and Dinah might create together. A family.

The one thing he believed he could not have.

Even if he figured out a way to spread himself thin enough to have a baby *and* a wife, Dinah was the wrong woman. Her focus was on her own career goals and Jenny. There was no room in her life for a husband.

He couldn't have it all.

After drying off with a huge towel, he collapsed

naked onto the bed. He flipped the blankets over himself and stared up into the darkness.

"He couldn't have it all," echoed in his mind. And so, he couldn't have Dinah. He couldn't have Jenny. He would turn his back on the woman he loved and proceed with his plans to adopt a child. A child who wouldn't be Jenny.

He pressed the heels of his hands to his throbbing temples. "Hell," he muttered, then gave in to the exhaustion that crept over him.

"Did we sleep well?" Dinah said as she zipped Jenny into a playsuit. "That's dumb, Jenny, the way I say 'we' when I talk to you. You're a person in your own right. You even have an opinion about broccoli. You slept like a log. I slept terribly, tossing and turning. There will be no more of this 'we' nonsense."

"Dada," Jenny said. "Da."

"Shh, sweetie. It's very early, but I know you're hungry. We're going to sneak downstairs and feed you without waking Preston."

Not because she selflessly wanted Preston to sleep longer, she added to herself. She simply wasn't ready to face him yet. Confusion was swirling through her mind with ever-increasing force, while her heart shouted questions she didn't want to hear. She was a wreck, an emotional mess.

She pulled the sash of her rose-colored satin

robe tight, then picked up Jenny and left the bedroom. As she headed for the stairs, she glanced back at the closed doors along the hall, wondering where Preston was sleeping.

"Dada," Jenny said.

"Shh."

Preston's house was lovely, Dinah mused as she went down the stairs. It was large, with plenty of windows to allow the sunshine to pour in and make the rooms bright and cheerful.

It was a perfect home for a family, and like a masochistic fool she'd fantasized in the night about what it would be like to be there permanently as Preston's wife, with Jenny as their daughter.

Ridiculous, she chided herself. Why would her mind travel down such a whimsical path when she didn't even know if she was in love with Preston? Why would she daydream about being his wife? Absurd. She had no space in her life for Preston, and he had no desire to have a wife. A child, yes. A wife, no. He didn't want a complete family.

"So shape up your mind, Dinah," she muttered.

"Dada!" Jenny exclaimed.

"You're a big help," Dinah said, then kissed Jenny on the forehead.

She was halfway across the living room, when the doorbell rang. Gasping in surprise, she turned toward the front door.

Who on earth would be ringing the bell so early?

she wondered. Should she open the door? Go wake Preston? No, that was silly. She was perfectly capable of answering a door.

"Sit for a second, sweetheart," she said, placing Jenny on the floor.

She checked the front of her robe to be certain it was completely closed, then hurried to the door and opened it. Her eyes widened as she found herself staring at an attractive young woman whose expression reflected her own surprise at seeing Dinah.

"Oh," they said in unison.

The woman regained her composure before Dinah did.

"I'm terribly sorry," she said. "I was writing a note on this envelope, and inadvertently leaned on the doorbell. I realize it's very early, but I'm going into the office before normal hours to catch up on my paperwork. Oh, I should introduce myself. I'm Betty Cushman. I've been assigned as Dr. Harper's caseworker from social services."

Oh, no, Dinah thought frantically. This was the woman who would be investigating Preston, writing reports on whether or not he would be a proper single father. And there she stood in her robe, having obviously just gotten out of bed.

"Good morning," Dinah said, managing a small smile. "I'm—"

Before she could continue, Preston came barreling down the stairs wearing only his jeans. His hair was tousled, and a dark shadow of beard covered the lower half of his face. He strode across the room to Dinah and placed his hands on her shoulders, looking over her head at Betty Cushman. Betty introduced herself, and his fingers tightened on Dinah's shoulders.

"It's nice to meet you," he said, then cleared his throat.

"I was going to leave this envelope under your mat," Betty said. "These papers should have been included in the packet you already received. I'm very sorry I rang the bell and . . . disturbed you. I'll be on my way now. Good-bye."

Preston took the envelope. "Well . . . yes, good-bye, Miss Cushman."

Betty Cushman left, and he had to move a very stiff Dinah backward so he could shut the door. "Oh, boy," he said, dragging one hand through his hair.

Dinah spun around and flattened her hands on his chest. The feel of his warm, bare skin momentarily distracted her. Her hands started to slide across his chest, fingers teasing through the dark hair, but she caught herself in time.

"Preston!" she exclaimed. "That was your caseworker from social services. Do you realize what this means?"

"She's very dedicated to her job to go into the office so early?" he asked with a rather weak smile.

"Would you wake up, please? Betty Cushman will be writing a report on you. Your front door was opened by a woman wearing only a robe. A woman who obviously spent the night here. What kind of father does that make you?"

A grin spread across his face, and he trapped her hands on his chest with his own.

"A healthy one," he said.

She attempted to pull her hands free, but he tightened his hold. She could feel the taut muscles beneath her palms, the warm, tempting skin. Heat flowed up her arms and danced across her breasts, making them yearn for Preston's soothing, sensual touch.

"Ah, Dinah," he murmured, lowering his head toward hers.

"Dada!" Jenny suddenly cried.

He jerked his head around to see Jenny crawling across the room toward them. Sighing, he looked back at Dinah for one long, heart-stopping moment, then released her, and went to Jenny. He scooped the baby up off the floor.

"Hi, Munchkin. How's my girl?"

She laughed and patted him on the nose. "Dada."

"You've got great taste in noses, Jenny," he said, smiling at her.

"Preston?" Dinah asked, trying to get back to the serious issue at hand. "Do you realize what I've done by answering your door dressed like this? Miss Cushman will put it in her report that you have women who . . . Social services might decide that this isn't the proper environment for a child to grow up in. Oh, Preston, if you're denied your baby because of this, because of me, I'll never forgive myself."

"Whoa," he said. "Let's not jump to world-shattering conclusions. Did you come down here this early to feed Jenny?"

"Yes."

"Well, take her out into the kitchen and get her some breakfast. I'll call my attorney and ask him if this means I'm in trouble with social services. Go on. Jenny is hungry."

"All right." She crossed the room and took Jenny from him. "Will you tell me exactly what your attorney says about this?"

He nodded. "Yes."

"You know, I could go to social services. I could explain about the water sprinklers in my apartment, and that you were simply offering Jenny and me shelter. I'll make them understand."

"You're getting ahead of yourself again. Go feed Jenny while I call Jack." He smiled at her, drawing one thumb over her cheek. "Go on."

Their eyes met for a moment, then Dinah whirled, starting toward the back of the house, where she assumed the kitchen was.

Once Dinah was out of sight, Preston sank onto the sofa and picked up the telephone. He dialed Jack's home number and waited for him to answer.

"What? Yeah? Who?"

"So much for my lawyer being always on the ball," Preston said. "Wake up, Jack. It's Preston."

"Preston? Do you know what time it is? Don't tell me. You went and got yourself arrested, and I have the dubious honor of being the recipient of your you-may-make-one-telephone-call call, right?"

"No, I'm not in jail, F. Lee Bailey. Jack, wake up and listen."

"Okay, okay. But you're asking a lot from a man who hasn't had any coffee yet."

Preston began by telling Jack who Dinah and Jenny were, then went on to explain the water damage in Dinah's apartment and her subsequent meeting of Betty Cushman.

"So, tell me, Jack," he finished, "is this going to reflect badly on my application at social services?"

"Hell, I don't know," Jack said, obviously now wide awake. "You're a red-blooded male. They can't expect you to live like a monk." He paused. "Then again, there are so many people who want babies, you could possibly be disqualified over an episode like this."

"Lord, you're cheerful. You're not doing a whole helluva lot for my morale, Jack."

"I call 'em as I see 'em. Let me do some checking and try to find out what social services' attitude is about this type of thing."

"Get back to me as quickly as possible, will you? Dinah is very upset about what happened.

She blames herself for opening the door dressed in her robe. She has enough to deal with right now, and I don't want her caused further distress over this."

"Your machismo is showing," Jack said, chuckling. "I do believe I hear a bit of the male beast protecting his lady. Try to forget the whole thing for now. You have enough on your mind too, Preston."

"I do?"

"Harper, you and I go way back. I know you as well as I do my own brother. I've been sitting here—well, actually I'm sprawled on my bed as my wife snoozes blissfully on—while you've been talking about Dinah. Preston, you've got heart trouble. I have five that will get me ten that says you're in love with her."

"Are you out of your tiny mind?" Preston exclaimed. "All I did was tell you what was going on here."

"Yes, but I heard the tone of your voice when you talked about Dinah. And Jenny too. Those two have got you, boy, and I think it's great. You're long overdue."

"Jack, I have my life mapped out. I'm going to adopt my baby and go from there."

"We'll see. May I go back to sleep now? My alarm isn't set to go off for another hour."

"What? Oh, sure. Thanks for your help."

"Preston?"

"Yes?"

"Are you in love with Dinah?"

Preston hesitated a moment, then sighed. "Yes, I am, but it won't work, Jack. She's devoted to Jenny and to her career. I know it, and I'm accepting it."

"We'll see."

"Would you quit saying that?"

"Good-bye, Preston. Have a nice day. Oh, I'm billing you for this consultation."

"Do so," Preston muttered, then hung up on the sound of Jack's laughter.

Preston stared into space for a long moment, trying to forget he'd just admitted to Jack that he loved Dinah. It didn't work. There was no escaping from the fact that he'd fallen in love with her, and he'd like to wring his own neck for having let down his emotional guard.

"Dada," Jenny greeted him as he entered the kitchen. She pounded on the table. "Toe."

He smiled. "Yes, I see you're having toast."

"Open," Dinah said, and spooned some soft-boiled egg into Jenny's mouth. Jenny was sitting in a captain's chair by the table with Dinah in another right in front of her so that the baby couldn't topple off. "Yummy egg, Jenny."

Dinah and Preston laughed together, then their eyes met again. Their smiles faded as memories of their magical evening flooded through their minds, bringing with them hot, insistant desire.

Finally Dinah tore her gaze from his, cleared her throat, and spooned more egg into Jenny's mouth.

"What did your attorney say?" she asked, keeping her attention focused on Jenny.

About what? Preston wondered hazily, staring at Dinah. Oh, right. "He said he really doesn't know what social services' stand is on something like this. He's going to do some checking and see what he can find out."

"What do *you* think?"

He shrugged. "I don't have the foggiest idea. Try to put the whole thing out of your mind for now."

She sighed. "I'll try."

"I'm going to shower and dress. I want to stop by the hospital first and check on a patient. He's a toddler who nearly drowned, and he's not responding as well as I'd like."

Dinah looked up at him. "You're a wonderfully dedicated doctor, Preston. I respect that very much."

"Well, a person can easily grow tired of that dedication when it disrupts her personal life. I continually have to cancel, or cut short, social outings, quiet evenings at home, things like that. I've long since accepted my life the way it is because I chose it. I wouldn't expect anyone else to."

"You'll be asking the child you adopt to understand."

"Well, yes, because I'll make sure I make it up to

her . . . or him. I can handle that. But there isn't enough hours for private time with a wife, as well as father-and-child time." He turned and started toward the door. "I can't have a complete family. I can't have it all, especially if my wife is pursuing a career of her own. The whole scenario is totally impossible."

"I think you're wrong," she said.

He stopped and looked back at her. "What?"

"Never mind. It just popped out of my mouth. I didn't even realize I was thinking that. It's none of my business."

"Why do you think I'm wrong?"

"No, Preston, I was out of line. You and I feel the same about our careers. That's what's so ridiculous about what I said. I thoroughly agree with you that anyone's life can be sliced into only so many pieces. It's just that . . ." Her voice trailed off.

"That?" he prompted.

"I don't know," she said with a little shrug. "My initial reaction to what you said was that if your wife truly loved you as you did her, understood you as you did her, then you could *both* have it all. Your life together would be based on a strong foundation, and workable compromises could always be reached."

Preston frowned, and she shook her head.

"I sound like something out of a book like the one about babies that I keep close to my fingertips. It's easy to print it on paper, but quite another thing to actually live it. No, you're right, Preston. Your life and mine are both full enough."

"But . . ." he started. But what? He loved her, so there had to be a way to make room for each other? No, it couldn't be done. He'd known that for a long time. "I'm going to take a shower." He turned and strode from the room.

Dinah watched him go, and a wave of icy misery seemed to sweep over her. She jumped in surprise, when Jenny tugged a lock of her hair. "Ready for a bottle, sweetheart? Bottle?"

When Preston emerged from his bedroom twenty minutes later, he met Dinah and Jenny in the hallway.

"Listen," he said, "as soon as I get home tonight, we'll go over to your apartment and see what the management is planning to do about the water damage. It's going to take a while to dry things out and have repairs done. We'll have the weekend to move Jenny's crib, high chair, and whatever, over here."

"Preston, I think Jenny and I should go to a hotel. You've been wonderful, but we're disrupting your routine and—"

"No, no, this is good practice for me. You know, having a baby in the house."

"But what will social services think?"

"I'll explain it to them if they ask. Besides, Betty Cushman has already seen you here. Your moving to a hotel isn't going to erase what happened this morning. Look, this is much better. My housekeeper comes in twice a week to clean, and she makes casseroles that she puts in the freezer. There's plenty of food all set to go. The nurses at the hospital are planning Clancy's retirement party, so she ought to be available next week. This is the best place for you and Jenny to be."

"But . . ."

"That's settled. I'm off to the hospital. Have a good day at the office, ladies." He strode past them and bounded down the stairs.

"But . . ." Dinah said again. "Well, for heaven's sake."

"Dada!" Jenny yelled happily.

Six

On Saturday Preston borrowed a pickup truck from a fellow doctor, and he, Dinah, and Jenny drove to Dinah's apartment.

A letter from the manager was attached to her door. He expressed his regret over the unfortunate accident with the water sprinklers, promised all damage would be repaired as quickly as possible, and urged the tenants to keep in touch so they'd know when they could move back in.

With a sense of dread Dinah inserted her key in the door, then looked up at Preston, who was holding Jenny. Her troubled gaze was met by smiles from the two. To her amazement, her own smile in return was genuine, and the cloud of depression that had settled over her dissipated as quickly as it had come.

Priorities, she thought as they entered the apartment. The majority of her material possessions had been destroyed, but the two most important *people* in her life were well and happy.

"Ah, progress," Preston said, glancing around the living room. "They've dried the carpet and a lot of your furniture is gone. The furniture went to the furniture hospital, Jenny," Preston said. "It's going to be fixed up as good as new."

"Ga," Jenny said. "Ga-Ga-Ga."

Dinah and Preston laughed, and with amazing cheer they collected what Dinah wanted to take to Preston's house.

Back there, they put together Jenny's crib, then Preston went to the store to purchase a new crib mattress while Dinah unpacked her and Jenny's clothes. By early evening everything was accomplished. They had a light supper of grilled cheese sandwiches and soup, then went into the living room.

"I'm exhausted," Dinah said, sinking onto the sofa. Jenny sat on the floor with an assortment of toys. "Moving is *not* fun."

Preston settled into his leather chair. "True, but it was necessary, and we got the job done."

"Preston, I don't know how to thank you for—"

He raised one hand to silence her. "Don't start with the thank-you thing, Dinah. I'm doing what

I want to do. I care about you and Jenny, remember? This is what it's all about, when you care. I'm no expert on the subject, but this all feels very right to me, so there's no reason to thank me."

Dinah nodded slowly. Yes, she thought, it *did* feel right, being there with Preston and Jenny, all three of them in a house that was truly a home. Oh, Dinah, be careful. She mustn't allow that ember of hope for a future with Preston to grow. This was all temporary, only for now, and she *must* remember that.

"Dada," Jenny said, crawling toward Preston.

He lifted her onto his lap. "How's my best girl in the whole world? You worked hard today, didn't you, Munchkin? I'd better get you to bed early tonight, kiddo. Hey, don't frown at me. I'm putting you to bed early because I love you, Jenny. You bet." He smiled at her. "Let's see what you've learned. Where's your nose?"

Jenny laughed, and Preston placed her tiny finger on her nose. As the game continued, Dinah got up, mumbling that she'd clean the kitchen, then she hurried from the room.

Leaning against a counter in the kitchen, she drew a deep breath. She felt disoriented, as though in a blink of an eye she'd become invisible. Preston had centered his attention on Jenny, telling the baby that he loved her and that *he*, not he and Dinah, would put her to bed.

Dinah's sense of peace and well-being had been

shattered. She felt totally excluded, like excess baggage. Jenny was Preston's best girl in the whole world, her mind repeated, and he loved her. And Dinah? Was she nothing more to Preston than a means for him to be with Jenny?

"I'm going to give Jenny her bath," he called from the living room. "Would you fix her bottle in a bit, Dinah?"

"Yes," she answered.

Was she behaving like a spoiled child? she asked herself as she loaded the dishwasher. Was she throwing a mental tantrum because a baby was receiving more attention than she? Was she reacting badly because Preston had told Jenny he loved her, while Dinah ached to hear him say those words to *her*?

This was all so confusing, she thought. Painful doubts were nagging at her, doubts about Preston's motives for moving her and Jenny into his home. He continually said that he *cared* for them, but he'd told Jenny he *loved* her. Was her mind taking her down a ridiculous road, or was she now seeing things clearly, as they really were? Was Preston's focus entirely on Jenny?

"Bottle ready?" Preston asked from the kitchen doorway.

"Oh," Dinah said, snapping herself out of her gloomy reverie. "I'll fix it right now."

"Are you all right, Dinah? You look pale."

She forced a smile. "I'm just tired. I'll be going to bed early tonight too."

Preston nodded, then returned to his leather chair with a freshly bathed Jenny on his lap. Lord above, he thought, what he wouldn't give to have Dinah going to bed early with *him*, making love with him, sleeping close to him throughout the night.

He wanted to tell her—hell, he wanted to shout out—that he loved her. But what was the point in declaring his love for a woman who didn't love him? What sense was there in asking her to share his life when she already had her own life mapped out the way she wanted it? Damn, what a mess. What a complicated, seemingly unsolvable mess.

Dinah entered the living room and handed Preston the warm bottle. As she sat on the sofa, flipping through a medical journal, she stole glances of Preston and Jenny from beneath her lashes.

They were so beautiful together, she mused yet again. They truly looked like father and daughter, and with every passing minute she was feeling more and more left out . . . and lonely. She had to stop thinking about all of this, about whether or not Preston cared only for Jenny, before she thoroughly depressed herself.

Just as Jenny finished her bottle, the telephone rang. Preston picked up the receiver, and Dinah took Jenny upstairs as he talked. After settling Jenny in bed, she returned to the living room.

Preston smiled at her as she curled up on the end of the sofa, though he wished she were curling up in his lap. It felt like years since he'd last kissed her, but he was wary of making any overt moves until she felt more comfortable in his home.

"That was Clancy," he said. "She'd been trying to reach you at your apartment, so I told her what was going on. She'll start coming here on Monday to day-sit for Jenny, because today was her last day at the hospital."

"Oh, that's wonderful news," Dinah said. "I won't worry about Jenny for a second, knowing she's here with Clancy."

"Good. Would you like to watch a movie on the VCR?"

She glanced at her watch. "There's a documentary coming on television in a few minutes about a sunken ship that's been discovered. I thought that sounded interesting."

"A sunken ship is interesting?" he said skeptically. "Well, okay, we'll watch the documentary."

"No, Preston, not if you'd rather see a movie."

"No problem. We'll compromise. We'll check out the ship, then pick a movie afterward. There. See how easily things can be solved with compromise?"

She picked an imaginary thread off her jeans. "Not everything," she said quietly. Smile, Dinah, she told herself, and looked at Preston. "As a contract attorney, I've long since learned that there are some areas that are etched in stone, with no compromise possible."

"I suppose. What made you decide to specialize in contract law?"

She smiled. "It's so challenging. Each new contract is like a puzzle, waiting for the pieces to be sorted out one by one. Sometimes I negotiate for days over a phrase, even a single word. I did a contract a few months ago in which . . ."

As Dinah chattered on, Preston watched her intently. She was so vibrantly alive, he mused, her eyes sparkling, her voice excited as she spoke of her work.

Whether she was discussing her career or tending to Jenny, she gave it her all. And that was how she would love, he was certain of it. She would give of herself totally, unconditionally, for all time. And, oh, Lord, how he wanted her love to be directed at him.

As she continued to talk, he listened, asking questions, making comments, storing away all the details he was learning about her profession because it was a part of who she was. It was important to her and, therefore, important to him.

"Uh-oh," he said finally.

"What's wrong?"

"Look at the time. The documentary about the sunken ship is over."

She laughed. "You're tricky, Harper. You didn't

want to see it, so you got me talking about my job. Very clever."

He splayed one hand over his heart. "I'm innocent. Hey, I'm really into sunken ships."

"Ha!"

Their mingled laughter danced through the air, then faded as their eyes met. Desire began to throb deep within Dinah, and she looked away, fiddling with a throw pillow.

"I think I'll go on to bed," she said, her voice unsteady. "I'm very tired."

As she stood up, so did Preston. He walked over to her and placed his hands on her shoulders.

"How would you like to go to the beach tomorrow afternoon?" he asked. "We'll take a picnic and get Jenny a bright red pail and shovel. It'll be a—a family outing. Okay?"

"A family outing," she said slowly. "Yes, that sounds lovely. It's been so long since I've been to the beach. It will be a new experience for Jenny too. The book says it's vitally important that she continually have new experiences. It's a marvelous idea, Preston."

"Then we'll do it. Now, you get some sleep." He brushed his lips over hers. "I'll see you in the morning."

She nodded, then started across the room. At the bottom of the stairs she stopped and looked back at him.

"Thank you, Preston, for everything. I know you

said not to say thank you, but I have to. You are, without a doubt, the best friend I've ever had. Good night."

He watched as she disappeared up the stairs, then slouched down into his leather chair.

"The best friend she'd ever had," he repeated. That, according to Jack, was the foundation on which a solid marriage was built. Was it possible that Dinah might come to love him, Preston Harper, her best friend? Would her feelings for him grow into love, as his had?

Oh, hell, what was he thinking? Why had he suggested a "family outing"? He was starting to act and think like a man who believed he could have it all.

He leaned his head back and stared at the ceiling.

He *wanted* it all. He wanted Dinah as his wife, Jenny as his daughter. He and Dinah could work it out, compromise.

He was totally revamping his thinking on the subject, he realized, but, damm it, he was in love. The image of a future without Dinah was bleak and empty, cold and lonely.

With hard work, trust, understanding, and love, they could have it all.

But only if Dinah loved him as he loved her.

He narrowed his eyes. Okay, the battle was on. He would win Dinah's love. Somehow.

With a weary sigh he got to his feet and headed for the kitchen in search of something to eat.

• • •

The next day seemed to be encased in a rosy cocoon. The weather was warm and the sky a bright blue, dotted with marshmallow clouds. Gloomy thoughts were pushed aside and smiles were quick to appear.

Preston's beeper was mercifully quiet, and no emergencies pulled him back to the hospital after his usual rounds. At the beach Jenny allowed him to assist her in building a sand castle, which she promptly destroyed with her new red shovel.

Dinah laughed in delight. "I don't think Jenny understands the principle of the project."

"Maybe she's going to be part of a demolition crew when she grows up," Preston said. "I'm taking this very personally, you realize, Jennifer. That sand castle was one of my better efforts."

Jenny gave the demolished castle another whack with her shovel.

"It's gone, gone, gone," Dinah said, still laughing.

He stood up. "Well, ladies, I've worked up an appetite with my construction, and the destruction of my construction. I vote we eat."

"Sold," Dinah said. "All this fresh air has really made me hungry. This is a lovely spot you found, Preston. It's like being on a private beach here beside these big rocks. There were a lot of people on that stretch we passed, but no one has even strolled by here."

"Stick with me, kid," he said, wiggling his eyebrows. "I know what I'm doing." Now, that, he thought dryly, was the joke of the year. His future, which a week ago had been as clear as the sunny day they were enjoying, was now a cloudy haze of unknowns. He knew what he wanted. What was just beyond his reach was the knowledge of how to obtain it—Dinah's love. "Are you holding that food for ransom?"

"Coming right up, sir," she said, reaching for the picnic basket they'd packed earlier. "Your wish is my command."

Hey, now, he thought, that would solve his problems. *Dinah, I command you to fall in love with me.*

"Preston?"

"What? Oh." He took the ham sandwich she was offering him. "Thanks."

The basket also produced potato chips, fruit, drinks, and cookies. Jenny ate finger food from a plastic bowl, polishing off tiny pieces of ham, cheese, and fruit. Preston held a small plastic glass of apple juice to her lips.

"Hooray," he said. "Look at my big girl drinking out of a glass. I swear, I have the smartest Munchkin in the state of Florida."

Dinah stared at him, her appetite suddenly gone. There it was again, she thought. Preston was speaking in the singular, as though Jenny were exclusively his. And where did that leave Dinah

Bradshaw? No, she wasn't going to dwell on that today, not during this "family outing."

She was going to savor these hours, even if it was risky, even if the ember of hope within her was flickering into a flame.

"Preston," she said, forcing her dangerous thoughts aside, "has your attorney found out anything from social services about my being at your house the other morning?"

"No. They're very silent people over there. Jack couldn't get any information out of them." He paused. "No heavy talk today, okay, Dinah? Let's just enjoy ourselves."

"All right."

Preston offered Jenny more to drink. "The tummy is full," he said, "and madam is getting crabby. Nap time, Munchkin."

He spread a crib blanket next to the bigger one he and Dinah were sitting on. Laying Jenny on her stomach, he rubbed her back and told her a story about Gerald Giraffe, who wore twenty-two bow ties on his long neck. Within minutes Jenny was asleep.

"I've lost my audience," he said, and moved to sit next to Dinah. "Maybe my stories are boring."

She smiled. "They're wonderful stories."

"Why, thank you, ma'am." He turned his head to gaze at her intently. "Did you know that you have the most expressive eyes I've ever seen?"

"Well, I . . . no."

"You do." He slid one arm across her shoulders and lowered his head toward hers. "And the most kissable lips."

"I—"

"Which I'm about to kiss."

Thank goodness, she thought, and wrapped her arms around his neck.

The kiss was gentle, and sweet, and sensuous. It was the meeting of lips and tongues, and an igniting of desire that caused their hearts to race and heat to consume them.

They drew air into their lungs, then sought the other once again. Preston lowered her to the blanket, one of his legs across both of hers. The kiss deepened, growing hungry and urgent. One of his hands sought her breasts beneath her terry-cloth top, and a purr of pleasure escaped from her throat.

She rubbed her hands across his broad, muscular back, loving the strength of him, urging him closer. She wanted him, ached for him, the feel of his arousal against her forcing aside all of her doubts.

Preston drank in the essence of Dinah. His body tightened as blood pounded in his veins. He wanted her with a fierceness he'd never known before. He wanted to make love with the woman he loved. He wanted Dinah Bradshaw now and forever.

He tore his mouth from her and buried his face in the silken cascade of her hair.

"Preston?" she whispered.

"Shh. No," he said hoarsely. "Don't move. Give me a minute."

As he struggled for control, Dinah closed her eyes, waiting for the heat of desire within her to cool even as she relived the ecstasy of their kisses.

How she wanted to make love with Preston, to be one with him in a glorious union. She would close a door against all the confusion and doubts, not allowing them to enter the wondrous place that would belong only to her and Preston. She'd reach for him and—

He lifted his head, and she opened her eyes, bringing herself from her sensual reverie.

"As they say in the movies," he murmured, forcing a smile, "this isn't the time or the place." His smile faded. "Dinah, I do want you. You must know how much I want you. And you want me too."

"Yes. Yes, I do, but . . ."

"But." He nodded. "Life isn't that cut and dried right now, is it? Just don't forget that. . . ." *I love you.* No, he couldn't tell her yet. He could sense that this wasn't the time. "I care deeply for you. You will remember that, won't you?"

"Yes. I have . . . strong feelings for you too, Preston."

"Fair enough." He moved off her and sat up, wrapping his arms around drawn-up knees.

Dinah struggled to an upright position, then finger-combed her hair.

They sat quietly, side by side, staring out at the calm ocean, lost in their own thoughts. Yet each was very aware of the other.

When Jenny woke from her nap, they took her to the water so she could wiggle her toes in the lapping waves. Her piercing wail made it quite clear she didn't like this new bathtub, thank you very much, and they quickly returned to the blankets.

Another sand castle was built, and was immediately destroyed by a gleeful Jenny. Preston moaned. Dinah laughed.

In the late afternoon a brisk wind came up, and Preston scanned the sky.

"Dark clouds are rolling in fast," he said. "I think rain is heading this way."

Dinah glanced up. "You're right. The temperature is dropping too."

He looked directly at her, holding her gaze. "Dinah," he said in a low voice, "let's go home."

Seven

At home, Dinah and Preston made and ate dinner, played with Jenny, then prepared the child for bed. But beneath the surface of what appeared to be a perfectly normal evening was a crackling tension, a sensual web that was spinning tighter and tighter around them.

Whenever their eyes met or their hands inadvertently touched, an electric current seemed to shoot between them, arousing the desire swirling through their bodies.

The threatening clouds that had sent them scurrying from the beach eventually produced a driving rain with a biting wind. As Dinah carried Jenny up to bed, Preston built a fire in the enormous stone fireplace in the living room. The leap-ing orange flames welcomed her when she returned.

She sat down on the sofa, then sprang to her feet to restlessly pace the room. Preston set the fire screen back in place, then turned to look at her.

"Dinah?"

She halted her trek on the far side of the room from him and faced him.

"Are you all right?" he asked quietly.

"What? Oh, yes, I'm fine. It's just that some-times everything catches up with me. So much has happened so quickly, my world has been turned upside down, and . . . I go for days adapt-ing, adjusting, and then suddenly it all becomes so incredibly heavy, like a crushing weight and . . . oh, ignore me. I'm just in a very strange mood tonight."

He opened his arms to her. "You sound like someone who needs a hug. Come here."

And she went.

As naturally as taking her next breath, she stepped into Preston's embrace. His arms closed around her, pulling her to him. She savored the heat from his body as it warmed the chill of doubts and questions within her.

Let's go home, Preston had said, she thought. And she *was* home. There in that house, nestled against Preston, she was home.

And she loved him.

Oh, yes, she was deeply, irrevocably in love with Preston Harper.

How easy it would be, she mused, to tell herself that she *wasn't* in love with him. She was grateful to him for being there for her. She was exhausted and shouldn't be held responsible for nonsensical thoughts. She was mistaking lust for love. Yes, for desire like none she'd experienced before. With little effort she could rationalize away the truth she had at last allowed to surface.

But that wouldn't change her love. She was, indeed, in love with Preston.

Even as the flame of hope for a future with this man flared brighter, her logical mind told her she was in love with the wrong man, at the wrong time, in the wrong place.

And it was that last straw that suddenly made everything too much to bear. Dinah burst into tears.

"Dinah!" Preston exclaimed. He eased her away from him, his hands on her shoulders. Concern was etched on his face as he stared at the tears streaming down her pale cheeks. "Don't cry. Okay, Dinah? Everything is going to be fine, you'll see. If you cry, you'll mess up your sinus cavities and get a headache, and—and your nose will get all red and funny-looking. Please, don't cry."

"I'll cry," she said, continuing to do exactly that, "if I want to, Preston Harper. If you don't wish to subject yourself to looking at a funny red nose, then go away. I'm going to cry because I need to cry, because I'm an emotional wreck, and I've over-loaded my circuits. And because Mother Nature is a woman, and she gave the rest of us women the sense to know when we need to have a good cry so we can regroup and move forward. So, just—just shut up."

"Oh. Well . . . um, okay. That sounds reason-able, I guess. Sure it does." He wrapped his arms around her again and nestled her to him. "I'll hold you, and you cry for as long as you like. I won't say another word." He paused. "Would you prefer to sit down, or do you do your best crying standing up?"

Oh, how she loved his man, Dinah thought. He was trying so hard to be what he should for her while she cried. He was being so sweet and tender and dear, and she loved him so much, her heart actually ached with the realization of the depths of her feelings for him.

"Oh," she wailed, and buried her face in his shirtfront.

"There, there," he said, patting her on the back. "Just cry your little heart out, then you'll feel better. Except for your sinus headache, of course, but I'll bring you some aspirin for that when you've finished bawling . . . I mean, crying."

This was ridiculous, Dinah thought, sniffling. There was something absurd about having a good old-fashioned womanly cry when one had such an attentive audience. There she was in the arms of an incredibly handsome man, and she was soaking his shirt with salty tears.

She loved Preston Harper, and every hour, every second, she had with him was like a precious gem to be cherished. Yet there she stood wasting those moments by blubbering like an idiot. Enough was definitely enough.

She lifted her head and dashed the tears from her cheeks. "All done."

"Really? That wasn't much of a show. Your nose isn't even red."

She smiled. "Oh, Preston, I . . . I . . . you're a wonderful man, you truly are."

"You're pretty special yourself, Dinah Bradshaw."

He smiled, too, and their gazes held. But then their smiles faded as the ever-present desire within them burst into licking flames of heated passion, as real as the fire burning in the hearth.

"Dinah," Preston said with a groan, then he lowered his lips to hers, pulling her tight against him.

She answered the demands of his lips and tongue with an abandon that might once have shocked her. But not now, because this was Preston, and she loved him. The obvious hunger and want within him equaled her own. Her tongue found his, dueled with it, danced with a seductive rhythm that echoed the pulsing deep within her.

Reality fled, and there was only herself wanting, needing, this man.

"Dinah," he whispered, "I want to make love with you."

"Yes, Preston, I want you, too, and I promise I won't regret taking this step. I won't be sorry. But we mustn't forget that what we have together is temporary." Wasn't it? Or was there hope that maybe, just maybe . . . "We have to remember that this, all of it, is only for now."

Not a chance, sweet Dinah, Preston thought. He wouldn't let her go. She had enough to deal with at the moment, but when the time was right he'd tell her how he felt, convince her that they could have it all, together. She cared deeply for him, she considered him her best friend. She had only to take that last step and love him, forever.

"Preston, did you hear what I said?" she asked. It was temporary, she tried to convince herself, because Preston didn't want a wife. Oh, how she loved him. They *could* make it work, but . . . "Preston?"

"Yes, I heard you. You said that what we have is temporary, only for the here and now. I heard every word, Dinah."

He cradled her face in his hands, and their gazes held for a long moment. When Dinah shivered, he dropped his hands and encircled her with his arms.

Again he claimed her mouth in a searing kiss.

He could no longer think, but could only feel, and savor the woman in his arms. Heat gathered tight and urgent in his body, throbbing, demanding, causing his manhood to surge.

With a throaty groan he broke the kiss. Then with fumbling, eager hands, they shed their clothes to stand naked before each other. The glow from the fire poured over them like a golden waterfall, and he lowered her to the thick carpet, stretching out beside her.

"Dear Lord," he said, not recognizing his own voice, "you're exquisite. You're so beautiful, Dinah. So, so beautiful."

Her gaze skimmed over him, missing no detail of his taut, tanned body. He was perfectly proportioned, each part of him complementing the next. Dark curls covered his broad chest, then tapered to a narrow strip below his belly. His arousal was bold, declaring his desire for her.

Oh, Preston, she thought dreamily. There was only the now and what they would share. Nothing would intrude on the ecstasy they would find.

"You're magnificent, Preston," she whispered.

They wanted. They needed. They burned with desire. They kissed and touched, caressed, explored, and discovered, until their passion consumed them, and they could bear no more.

"Preston, please."

He shifted over her, catching his weight on his

forearms and weaving his fingers through her silken hair.

I love you, Dinah, he thought.

Oh, Preston, I love you so much, she thought.

"I want you," he said. "Now."

"And I want you. Now."

He entered her slowly, watching her face, until she sank her hands into his thick hair and urged his lips onto hers. He thrust his tongue into her mouth at the same moment he thrust his manhood deep within her body, filling her, making them one.

Their dance of love began with a cadence that was urgent, hungry, pounding like the wild storm raging outside. Their need overtook them as they moved perfectly together, the rhythm quickening as tensions built within them. Coiling tighter . . . tighter . . . lifting them up, up, up—

"Preston!"

"Oh, yes . . . Dinah."

They clung to each other as they were flung far beyond reality to a place neither had gone to before. They were suspended in a maelstrom of sensations and emotions, then drifted back slowly, sated, spent, awed.

With his last ounce of energy Preston moved off Dinah. He held her close, nestling her to his cooling body as he waited for his heart to stop racing and his breathing to return to normal.

Dear Lord, he thought, a strange ache in his

throat. Their lovemaking had been beyond his dreams in its beauty, its splendor. He had, for the first time in his life, made love with a woman he loved, and there were no words to describe the ecstasy of what they'd shared.

"Dinah," he said quietly, "thank you for . . . it was wonderful."

"Yes. Yes, it was. I've never felt so . . . words aren't necessary, Preston. We both know what we shared. We know."

They gazed into the hypnotizing flames of the fire, then their eyes drifted closed, and they dozed. Later, when they woke, Preston stood and reached down to Dinah. She placed her hand in his, and he pulled her to her feet.

Without speaking they went up the stairs and into his bedroom. Without speaking they reached eagerly for each other. Without speaking they soared beyond reality once again, meshed as one.

Then they slept, heads resting on the same pillow, the secret words of love echoing in their dreams.

When Preston woke the next morning, a light, easy rain was falling, and the bedroom was in semidarkness. Without opening his eyes, he slid one hand across the bed in search of Dinah. Finding nothing, he turned his head and opened his eyes.

Dinah? he thought in alarm, then realized she had no doubt gotten up to tend to a wet-diapered and hungry Jenny.

He laced his fingers beneath his head and stared up at the ceiling, savoring the memories of the lovemaking shared with Dinah.

He felt terrific, fantastic, but it went far beyond being physically satisfied. A sense of peace glowed warmly within him, intertwined with excitement, anticipation. The future held such promise of happiness, of completeness, of being half of a wonderful whole.

Because he was in love with Dinah Bradshaw, and she was, he was certain, in love with him.

Yes, he admitted to himself, she hadn't said the words, but the way she'd given of herself to him spoke volumes. He had to be patient, give her time to adjust to all the upheavals in her life, then reap the rewards of having not pushed or pressured her.

He flipped back the blankets and headed for the shower, a spring to his step and a smile on his face.

When Preston entered the kitchen, Dinah was lifting Jenny out of her high chair.

"Dada," Jenny said, extending her arms to him.

"Hello, Preston," Dinah said, smiling warmly. "There's coffee in the coffeemaker."

"Great."

He brushed his lips over Dinah's as Jenny patted him on the cheek, then he kissed Jenny on the forehead and set her on the floor.

"Now," he said, "we'll say good morning properly."

His gaze skimmed over Dinah, her enticing figure outlined by her robe, and he remembered how exquisite she'd been naked before him, then beneath him. He wove his fingers through her appealingly tousled hair, then brought his lips down to hers.

As she twined her arms around his neck, he dropped his hands to her back to press her close. Her breasts crushed against his chest, and he parted her lips to find her tongue.

Oh, good morning, my love, Dinah thought as heat spiraled within her.

She pressed into him, returning his kiss with total abandon, remembering their night, wanting more.

Suddenly a loud crash shattered the sensual spell weaving around them. They jerked apart, blinked, then turned their heads to find the source of the noise.

"Ga, ga, ga," Jenny said. She was surrounded by pots and pans, and was reaching into the lower cupboard for more.

Preston smiled. "Jenny, your timing is lousy." He gave Dinah another fast, hard kiss, then stepped over the collection of pots to pour himself a mug of coffee.

"Planning on baking something?" Dinah asked Jenny. "Or are you just redecorating? Jenny, you're really making a mess."

The baby smiled brightly.

"Good Lord!" Preston yelled. "What is this?"

Dinah jumped. "Heavens, you scared me. What is what?"

He peered into his coffee mug. "This . . . stuff."

"Oh, that's peppermint coffee. I brought it from my apartment."

"Peppermint coffee?" he repeated, still staring into the mug. "Peppermint? I want a good, strong cup of coffee in the morning to jump-start my system, not something that tastes like a liquid candy cane. This is awful."

She planted her fists on her hips. "Well, excuse me, doctor. I happen to be very fond of peppermint coffee, and since I was the one preparing it, the choice of flavor was mine to make."

"Dandy." He hunkered down and began to plow through Jenny's assortment of pots and pans. "There's an old coffeepot in here somewhere. I'm going to make some *real* coffee."

"What you're making," Dinah said with a little snort of disgust, "is a racket to go along with the tantrum you're throwing. I have never in my life seen anyone react so ridiculously over a cup of coffee."

"Here it is." He picked up a small coffeepot, then stood and glared at her. "Tantrum?"

"What would you call it?"

"I was merely expressing my opinion."

"Opinions can be expressed, sir, without being loud and rude." She crossed her arms and tapped one foot impatiently. "Fix your own dumb, boring, ordinary coffee."

"I intend to," he said, turning to the sink. He filled the pot with water and coffee and placed it on the stove. "There."

He looked at Dinah, and his frown slowly changed into a smile.

"His and her coffeepots," he said. "That solved that. What we have here is compromise in its purest form. I think maybe this is an example of the type of little adjustments people make when they get married and set up housekeeping together, don't you?"

Married? Dinah thought. Dear heaven, was the man peering into her brain? Did he see her love for him as clearly as a neon sign, and somehow sense that, yes, she wanted to marry him? No, no, he was just talking. His reference to marriage meant nothing.

"I . . . um, I'd better get dressed," she said.

"Leave Jenny here, and I'll watch her."

"Oh. Well, all right. Thank you. Clancy should be arriving soon."

"Hey," Preston said, "I apologize for pitching a fit about the coffee."

"No, it's my fault. I've been alone so long, I just didn't think about whether or not you'd like peppermint coffee."

"You're not alone anymore, Dinah," he said seriously.

Images of their lovemaking flitted through her mind. "No, I'm not alone. Not—not at the moment." She hurried across the room, then stopped by the door. "Preston?"

"Yes?"

"Your coffee would brew faster if you turned the flame on under the pot. Bye." She left the kitchen.

Preston chuckled and flipped the proper knob on the stove. Lord, he thought, how he loved his beautiful Dinah.

Jenny sent a lid flying across the room.

"Go for it, Munchkin. Messes can be fixed." He hoped. Because his relationship with Dinah was still in one helluva mess.

Just as Dinah was preparing to leave her office at the end of what had been an extremely hectic day, Preston telephoned to say he had an emergency and would be late getting home. Before she could say more than "Oh," he'd hung up.

When Preston entered the house shortly after seven o'clock, he found Dinah pacing the living room with Jenny on her hip. A legal-sized document was in her other hand and held at arm's length, away from a wiggling Jenny.

"Hi," he said. "What's going on?" His glance fell on a scattered pile of torn papers on the floor. "My medical journals? They were stacked on the end table and . . . that confetti is definitely my medical journals."

"Preston, I'm sorry," Dinah said wearily. "I've got to proof this contract tonight so it's ready for signatures first thing tomorrow morning. I had Jenny all set up on the floor with her toys because she totally rebelled against staying in her playpen and I couldn't concentrate with her yelling like that. I left the room to get some notes from my briefcase, but I swear I was gone only a couple of minutes. That's all it took. She destroyed the journals."

He nodded. "Munchkins move fast. Are you about finished with that contract?"

She sighed. "No. Jenny is being very demanding for attention tonight. I've just read the same paragraph three times and I'm still not positive as to what it says. This, obviously, is not working very well." She paused. "You must be starving. I had a salad for dinner, but you surely want something more substantial. I'd better go see what I can find for you to eat and—"

"Whoa. Dinah, you're not the maid. I'm perfectly capable of fixing myself something to eat.

You're also not Superwoman. No one could give their best effort to proofing an intricate contract while trying to tend to an active baby."

"Whenever I bring work home I start right in on it after I've eaten. Jenny just didn't cooperate."

"I think you'd better consider changing your routine. You know, doing your work after Jenny goes to bed." He shrugged. "It's just a thought. Tonight is now under control because I'm taking care of Jenny." He scooped the baby out of Dinah's grasp. "Right, Munchkin? We're a team, you and I. Come on. You can help me eat a peanut butter and jelly sandwich." He leaned over and kissed Dinah on the lips. "More of that later," he said, and started toward the kitchen. "The dynamic duo, Jenny, that's who we are, right? You bet. You're my number one Munchkin."

Dinah watched them go, a cold knot of apprehension tightening in her stomach. She had, she knew, totally blown her attempt to wear more than one hat at a time. Then, enter Preston, who'd immediately made order out of chaos. And who had spoken again as though Jenny were the only one he truly cared about.

People talked to babies all the time, Dinah reasoned. Was she reading too much into the actual words Preston said to Jenny? Was he just chattering to hold Jenny's attention, keep her entertained?

Dinah sank onto the sofa with a sigh, and forced herself to concentrate on the contract. Preston came back into the room a short time later, settling into his leather chair with Jenny on his lap. He read to her from a large storybook, keeping his voice as quiet as possible.

When the telephone rang twenty minutes later, Dinah gasped in shock at the sudden noise. Preston quickly picked up the receiver.

"Dr. Harper . . . I see . . . Yes, okay, Sharon, call the hospital and tell them I'm on my way. Thanks."

He dropped the receiver back into place and stood in the same motion.

"I'm sorry about this," he said to Dinah. "That was my answering service, and I have an emergency. I said I'd tend to Jenny so you could work, and now I'm bailing out on you."

"Good heavens, Preston, I understand. You have a patient who needs you. I'm going to give Jenny her bath and bottle, put her to bed, *then* tackle proofing the remainder of this contract. That's what I should have done in the first place. You'd better hurry. They're waiting for you. I'll be here when you get back."

Preston remained where he was, staring at her. He'd never dreamed that it was possible to love someone as much as he did Dinah Bradshaw.

"Ga, ga," Jenny said.

Dinah laughed. "Another voice heard from. Go, Dr. Harper."

He slid one hand around the nape of Dinah's neck and kissed her so deeply, so thoroughly, she was breathless and trembling when he released her. Then he gave Jenny a loud, smacking kiss on the forehead, handed the baby to Dinah, and strode from the room.

Dinah watched him go, not attempting to speak as she willed her heart to return to a normal tempo. The front door clicked shut, and she tightened her hold on Jenny.

"Oh, Jenny," she said, "I've never been so happy and so miserable in my entire life."

With a sigh she got to her feet and carried Jenny upstairs for a giggly romp in the bath.

When Preston returned home after eleven o'clock, he closed the door and stood statue still, drinking in the scene before him.

Dinah was curled up in his leather chair, her feet tucked beside her, a book opened on her knees. Her head was nestled in the chair's high side-wing, and the waning fire cast a soft golden glow over her. She was sound asleep.

He walked slowly toward her, his heart beating wildly. Not because of desire, but because of the deep love he felt for her.

To walk into that room and find her asleep in his chair, where she'd been waiting for him, brought an ache to his throat and a gentle touch to his soul. What had been chillingly empty was filled with warmth. What had been missing was now found.

He loved Dinah, and it was time that she knew his true feelings for her.

He leaned down to brush his lips over the soft, dewy skin of her cheek. She slowly opened her eyes, then a lovely smile formed on her lips.

Preston felt as though his heart would burst from the magnitude of his love for her.

"Hello," he said, his voice raspy.

"Hi." She yawned and stretched, then stood. "I dozed off, I guess. How's your patient?"

"Stable. He's a three-year-old boy who took a bad fall down a flight of stairs. He'll be all right."

"I'm glad." She turned to the fire and held out her hands to the heat. "The fire will be out soon, unless you want to add another log."

"No, it's late."

"True. I finished all the work I brought home. You'd think I would have had enough sense to wait until Jenny was in bed before I started it. Well, a lesson learned." She laughed softly. "My reference book didn't cover what to do about homework when the baby is still up."

"Dinah?"

"Yes?"

"Would you turn around and look at me, please? This is important."

She turned. "Yes?"

A trickle of sweat ran down Preston's back, and

a knot coiled in his stomach. "I intended to wait awhile before saying this to you because I felt you've had a great deal to adjust to very quickly. But I just can't do it. I can't keep silent any longer."

"Preston, what is it? You're so serious, you're frightening me."

"Frightening *you*? *I'm* the one who's scared to death. Maybe this is the wrong time to tell you, but I—" He stopped and drew a deep breath. "Dinah, I love you. You are my life, my best friend. Dinah, I love you so damn much."

Dinah leaned against the leather chair for support, afraid her trembling legs would give way beneath her. She felt the color drain from her face.

"What?" she whispered. "No, no, I heard what you said, but . . . Preston, you have your life all planned. You're going to adopt a baby through social services."

"No, I'm not, because I have Jenny now. Dinah, please, I know what I said about how my life was to be, but that was before you, before Jenny. We'll replan our lives, make this work for both of us. We *can* have it all."

"Preston, I—"

"But there's one thing missing here," he rushed on, "and that's how *you* feel about *me*. You have a plan for your life, too, and from everything you've said, it doesn't include a commitment with a man right now. I know you care for me, Dinah, but how much? I have to know if there's any chance at all for us to have a future together. Talk to me, Dinah, please."

Her voice quivered when she spoke. "Oh, Preston, I love you. I was going to cling to every precious moment we had together, keep the memories hidden safely in my heart forever when it was over. There aren't words . . . there just aren't . . . to tell you how deeply I love you."

"Oh, Dinah, come here."

She flung herself into his outstretched arms, burying her face in the crook of his neck. He held her so tightly she could hardly breathe as a shudder swept through his body.

Preston loved her, her heart sang. All her fantasies and whimsical daydreams had come true. Was this actually happening, or had she drifted off to sleep and would soon wake to face chilling reality?

Preston murmured her name and eased his hold on her enough to trail nibbling kisses along her throat. She could feel his heat, feel his arousal. . . .

Oh, yes, she was awake. She was totally aware of the desire pulsing deep within her, of the tingling in her breasts that yearned for Preston's soothing touch. He loved her, she loved him, and the future was no longer a bleak landscape of loneliness and tears. The tomorrows were theirs to have, and life was glorious.

She would *not* listen to the taunting doubts

about Preston's first priority seeming to be Jenny. Nothing was going to tarnish what she and Preston now had.

"I'm so happy," she murmured. "This is like a fairy tale come true."

"You're right. This is a very special night, a magical night."

"I love you, Preston Harper."

Through the hours of their special night, their magical night, they reached for each other, the embers of desire within them bursting into flames over and over. They dozed, only to awaken with the need to again give and receive their love.

The next morning Dinah Bradshaw and Preston Harper left the house hand in hand as sunshine poured over them. They greeted the day and the world with matching smiles.

They were in love, and the future was theirs, together. . . .

Eight

"I appreciate your meeting me for lunch, Dr. Harper," Betty Cushman said. "My schedule is as crowded as yours, and this way we can at least keep from starving to death."

Preston smiled at the attractive woman. "Yes, this is a good idea. It eases my guilt about not bringing social services up-to-date on the changes in my life since I applied to adopt a baby. This lunch is most definitely on me. Oh, and call me Preston."

"I'm Betty. So, you've told me that you're seriously involved with Dinah Bradshaw, who has guardianship custody of Jenny. This casts an entirely different light on your adoption application."

"I realize that, and I apologize for not informing

you immediately of my new circumstances. You're extremely busy, and I'm wasting your time."

"Not necessarily," Betty said.

"What do you mean?"

"You have no idea how difficult it is to find homes for older children who desperately need them. The majority of people applying to adopt a baby want a cuddly newborn, or at least an infant who isn't more than a few months old. The other children, the older ones, get caught in the foster-home shuffle. It's those kids that break my heart. Those are the ones I try so hard to place in permanent family environments."

"Go on," Preston said.

"I'm not asking you for a decision today because it's most definitely something you'll need to discuss with Dinah. All I'm requesting is that you allow me to keep your file open, with the hope that you and Dinah might consider adopting an older child later."

"I see."

"May I do that? Keep your file open?"

"Well . . . sure, I guess that would be all right."

"Terrific. Preston, this lunch is on me. You just brightened my day more than I can tell you. So! When's the big event?"

"Big event?"

"Your wedding. From the way you spoke, I assumed you and Dinah were planning on getting married as quickly as possible."

Preston stirred some sugar into his coffee . . . and stirred . . . and stirred. . . . Finally he looked at Betty again.

"I want to marry Dinah today. Yesterday even. But the truth of the matter is, I haven't exactly asked her."

"Tell me if this is none of my business, but I have to ask. Why on earth haven't you asked her?"

"Betty," he said, a bleak expression on his face, "you are looking at a coward. So much has happened so quickly to Dinah, including falling in love with me. I'm scared to death that she'll want to wait so she can be even more certain that we both can do justice to our careers, and properly tend to Jenny, and, well, have it all. I haven't broached the subject of marriage because I don't want to hear her say no."

"Men," Betty said with a click of her tongue. "Your rationale is so strange at times. Preston, for heaven's sake, Dinah loves you. Ask her to marry you, and get on with your lives."

"I will. Soon. It's only been a week since she told me she loved me. I mean, she's probably still getting used to the idea."

Betty leaned across the table toward him. "Preston, you're right. You're a coward."

"Thanks," he said miserably. "I really needed that."

"Propose to the woman."

"I will. Soon."

Betty rolled her eyes. "Men are sooo weird."

As soon as Preston entered the house that evening, a delicious aroma assailed him. Jenny was in her playpen, and clapped her hands when she saw him.

"Dada!" She pulled herself to her feet and leaned over the top of the playpen. "Dada."

This was what it was all about, he thought, then smiled as Dinah came out of the kitchen and started across the room toward him.

And there she was, he mentally went on, the woman he loved with every breath in his body. She was his other half, his very best friend. What would she say if he gathered his courage and asked her to marry him? Well, he was going to find out . . . soon.

"Hello, my darling," she said, moving into his embrace.

"Hello," he said, then kissed her.

"Dada!" Jenny yelled.

Dinah laughed and stepped back. "The Munchkin roars. You'd better go tickle her tummy before she tries to climb out of there. Dinner will be on the table in a few minutes."

"I love you, Dinah."

"That's good, because I love you too."

"Dada!"

"I'm coming, Munchkin. If your mother could keep her hands off me, I'd be over there by now, Jenny."

"Oh, for heaven's sake," Dinah said, laughing. "There's certainly nothing wrong with your ego."

"Why should there be? I have two lovely ladies demanding my attention the minute I walk in the door."

Dinah shook her head. "I'm going to go get dinner on the table."

He chuckled, then crossed the room and lifted Jenny into his arms.

"Hello, Munchkin. How's my best girl in the world? Did you find a job yet? Hey, listen, kid, there's no such thing as a free lunch. I knew this zebra once who went looking for work and he—"

"Dada," Jenny said, then whacked Preston on the nose.

In the kitchen Dinah frowned as she dished up the food.

So, okay, she told herself, Jenny was Preston's best girl, but Dinah was his *woman*. He loved her, she loved him, and everything was working out perfectly.

Except . . . why hadn't Preston asked her to marry him? They'd declared their love, made beautiful love every night, spoke of their glorious future together, but he'd never said one word about marriage.

It didn't make sense, she mused, carrying plates to the table. She knew Preston had been adamant about not wanting a wife, but everything was different now. Wasn't it? Of course it was. So, drat the man, why hadn't he brought up the subject of marriage? If he didn't do it soon, *she* would.

"My, my," she said, laughing softly, "I'm certainly getting brave and liberated." She walked to the living room doorway. "Dinner is ready."

Later that evening, when Elizabeth Harper telephoned, her first inquiry was about how Jenny was.

"Boy, oh, boy, Mother," Preston teased, "I can't remember when you were this concerned about *me*."

"The privilege of being a grandmother. I've waited a long time for this."

"All right, we'll humor you. What's on your mind, sweet Mama?"

"The hospital benefit dance at the country club Saturday night."

"Oh, hell," he said, frowning. "I forgot all about it. I've had the tickets for weeks, but—"

"Well, you've had a lot on your mind, dear. I just spoke with Clancy about our crafts for the bazaar later in the year, and she said she could baby-sit Jenny Saturday night. I have to be at the dance because I'm on the committee. You did promise to receive the check for the pediatric wing, plus give a nice little thank-you speech. I thought I'd better jiggle your memory on the subject."

"You're a peach," he said dryly. "Okay, Dinah and I will be there."

"Splendid. Good night, dear."

"Bye, Mother." He replaced the receiver and looked at Dinah.

"What's wrong?" she asked.

"Nothing really. I simply forgot about a hospital benefit dance Saturday night. I have to give a thank-you speech for a check the committee is presenting. Clancy can stay with Jenny. We'll have to dress to the nines. Do you mind going?"

"Not at all. It's sounds like a lovely evening, and according to my book, Jenny is more than old enough to adjust to changes in routine."

"I thought you'd thrown that book away."

"I just glance through it on occasion." She smiled. "But for the most part I'm relying on my own instincts as a mother, and your expertise as a father and doctor. I really don't need the book anymore."

"Lord, I love you."

"Well, I love you too." She stared into space. "Now, let's see. What knock-'em-dead dress should I wear Saturday night? Will you be in a tuxedo?"

"Yep. I'll pull the penguin suit out of the closet."

"Then I'd better be certain my dress is sensational."

The dress, Preston thought Saturday night, was definitely sensational.

He stood at the bottom of the stairs, dressed in his custom-tailored tuxedo, and watched Dinah slowly make her descent. His heart thundered, and heat gathered low and heavy within him as she drew closer.

The dress that Dinah wore was a floor-length red creation that molded to the gentle curves of her figure. Shimmering, iridescent silver sequins cascaded in a feathery motif down the dress and long sleeves. Her hair was a halo of strawberry-blond waves, and her green eyes seemed to sparkle as brightly as the sequins.

"Sensational," Preston said, then cleared his throat. "Dinah, you're beautiful."

She stepped off the stairs and smiled at him. "And you're the most gorgeous penguin I've ever seen."

"Oh, you're a handsome couple," Clancy said

from the sofa. "You look as though you just stepped off the pages of a fashion magazine."

Jenny crawled toward them.

"You're not going tonight, Munchkin," Clancy said, picking up the baby. "You and I are due to build a tower of blocks."

Jenny yelled.

"We're gone," Preston said, laughing.

"Good night, sweetheart." Dinah kissed Jenny on the cheek. "Preston, she feels a little warm. She refused to eat much dinner too."

He placed his hand on Jenny's forehead. "She's fine, Dinah. She's just still warm from her bath."

"Dada," Jenny said, reaching out to them.

"Shoo," Clancy said. "She's about to launch into a screaming, 'Don't leave me with this witch' performance."

Dinah and Preston laughed, then hurried out of the door.

The ballroom of the country club was enormous, and filled with people dressed in their finery. A band played on one side of the gleaming dance floor, and small tables covered in linen cloths edged the room. The crystal chandeliers were dimmed, appearing like twinkling stars in the heavens. An aura of festive excitement tinged the air.

As Dinah and Preston entered the room, a momentary hush fell over the crowd of people. Dinah's step faltered as she realized the majority of the throng had turned to look at them.

"Is my nose on upside down?" she asked Preston under her breath.

He smiled at her. "You're beautiful. You've taken their breath away."

As the people redirected their attention to what they'd been doing, Preston's words made Dinah smile with purely feminine pleasure.

They, she thought, had made An Entrance, just like in the movies. As a couple they were dashing, smashing, sensational. She *was* beautiful in her sparkly dress, and Preston was the most handsome, most magnificent man there.

What that tuxedo did for his gorgeous body and rugged, tanned face, she decided, should be against the law. Oh, she was feeling smug and womanly because Preston Harper loved *her*. What a wonderful evening this was going to be.

Preston introduced her to so many people, she soon gave up the attempt to remember names. They chatted with Elizabeth, who looked lovely in a mint-green gown, and who was on the arm of a distinguished gentleman with thick gray hair and a ready smile.

Dinah danced with half a dozen men, all of whom were pleasant and full of praise for Preston. Then Preston claimed her, and she floated across the floor in his arms.

"Are you enjoying yourself?" he asked.

"Oh, yes, very much."

"Good. I was afraid . . . well . . ."

She tipped her head back to look at him. "Afraid of what?"

"I don't know. It's just that everyone I've introduced you to has talked about me. Not one person has asked what *you* do. I thought that might be annoying."

"Oh. I hadn't even noticed that no one inquired about *my* profession. Tonight I'm Preston Harper's lady, being accepted into your world."

"And?" he asked, frowning slightly.

"It's marvelous. It doesn't diminish who I am, Preston, it adds another layer, another role. If we went to a social event made up of my attorney friends, the same thing would probably happen in reverse. Would that bother *you*?"

"Lord, no. I'm very proud of what you've accomplished in your career."

"And I'm proud of you. I'll be delighted to hear people singing your praises for the entire evening."

"Dinah, I love you."

He pulled her closer, and the music played on.

An hour later a man moved to a microphone in front of the band and called for everyone's attention. He thanked them for showing their support by being there and making the benefit a tremendous success. He then said that the check for the proceeds from the event would be accepted by Dr. Preston Harper on behalf of the pediatric staff of the hospital.

Preston squeezed Dinah's hand, then left her to make his way to the microphone. The applause was deafening, and Dinah scanned the crowd, nearly bursting with pride as she saw the admiration on the faces of everyone there.

". . . this generous donation," Preston was saying when she turned her attention back to him. "All doctors are fiercely loyal to their specialty, both in heart and mind. To me, the babies, the children, deserve every bit of knowledge and expertise we can obtain, along with a hefty dose of love. This check will enable us to continue to provide the finest care possible for our tiny patients. Thank you all very much."

Applause broke out once again. Preston moved away from the microphone and handed the check to a woman who stood nearby.

Oh, yes, Dinah thought, Preston was an excellent doctor and he loved his Munchkins. And Jenny was his favorite Munchkin, his best girl in the world, and he loved her.

A shiver coursed through Dinah as she watched Preston slowly wend his way back to her, people stopping him time and again to shake his hand.

She would not, she vowed, allow her doubts

and fears to spoil this night. They'd be married, and together with Jenny they'd be a family. They'd be married. . . . They'd be married. . . . Oh, dear Lord, why hadn't Preston asked her to marry him?

Stop it, Dinah, she told herself. She was *not* going to ruin this evening. She wasn't Cinderella, where everything fell apart at midnight. She and Preston had a wondrous future life together. They would have it all.

"Done," he said, finally reaching her. "Would you like some refreshments, or do you want to dance?"

She needed, she instantly knew, to be held in his arms, so his strength, his heat, could chase away the taunting voices in her mind.

"May I have this dance?" she said, managing to smile.

He took her into his arms. "This one, and every one."

During the following hours Dinah's lighthearted mood returned, and all her gloomy thoughts were swept away by Preston and the ongoing festive atmosphere of the ball.

Just before midnight she and Preston sat at one of the small tables, sipping punch and nibbling on delicious small sandwiches. Few people had left the dance in spite of the late hour.

"Everyone is having such a lovely time," she

said, her gaze flickering over the crowd. "Including me."

"And me," Preston said. "I usually leave these things as early as I can without appearing rude. But with you, we just might dance until dawn."

She laughed. "I'll have a conference with my feet and see if they're up to it."

"Dr. Harper?" a young man said, appearing at the table.

"Yes?"

"Telephone, sir. You can take the call in the corridor right outside the ballroom doors."

"Do you know who it is?"

"A woman named Clancy. She said it was imperative that she speak to you."

Dinah and Preston leapt to their feet in the same instant.

"Thank you," Preston said to the young man. "Come on, Dinah."

He took her hand and hurried across the crowded room, Preston mumbling "Excuse me" as he urged people out of the way. In the corridor he snatched the receiver up off the table. Dinah's gaze was riveted on his face.

"Clancy?" he said. "Yes . . . damn . . . liquid Tylenol? . . . Good . . . Chloramphenicol drops? . . . All right, Clancy, we're on our way." He hung up.

"Preston?" Dinah said, her voice faint.

"Jenny has a roaring ear infection and a high

fever. Clancy is very worried. Dammit, Dinah, we've got to get home to Jenny. Now!"

The drive to the house seemed to take forever. Neither Preston nor Dinah spoke. Preston concentrated on the traffic while Dinah stared at her hands clutched tightly in her lap. Every thought, every image in her mind, was of Jenny.

When they burst through the front door, Clancy was pacing the floor, holding a screaming Jenny. Preston strode across the room and took Jenny into his arms, Dinah hovering at his side.

"Hey, Munchkin," he said, "hang in there, kiddo. We'll get you fixed up just super-duper."

Jenny whimpered.

"I'm here, sweetheart," Dinah said. "Oh, Preston, she's so flushed. Her cheeks are bright pink."

"Nothing I've done has helped, Preston," Clancy said. "You know I'm not an alarmist, but I felt you should be here. This isn't just an ordinary ear infection. Her fever is too high and she's in too much pain."

"You're right," Preston said. "We'd better—"

Jenny suddenly stiffened in Preston's arms and screamed as though she'd been struck by a sharp object. Fluid ran from her ear and down her face.

"Oh, God," Preston whispered.

Dinah clutched his upper arm. "What is it?"

Jenny shuddered, sighed, then leaned her head wearily on Preston's chest. She stuck her thumb in her mouth.

"Preston?" Dinah said frantically.

He took her hand and held it so tightly, she winced.

"Jenny's eardrum has ruptured," he said.

Her eyes widened and she looked quickly at Jenny, then met Preston's troubled gaze again.

"I don't understand," she said. "She's quiet now."

"The pressure and pain were building, and she's gotten relief from it because the eardrum ruptured. She's comfortable for the moment, but the situation is extremely serious. Dinah, if Jenny doesn't receive the proper care, she could lose the hearing in that ear."

"Oh, God, no," Dinah cried, a wave of dizziness sweeping over her.

"Clancy," Preston said, "give me that blanket for Jenny there on the chair. Dinah and I will leave for the hospital. You call the country club and have Maggie O'Leary paged. She's at the dance, and she's the best there is in this field. Ask her to meet us at the hospital."

"Consider it done," Clancy said, handing Preston the blanket. "Go. Get Jenny the help she needs."

"Jenny?" Dinah said, stroking the baby's cheek with a trembling hand. "Oh, Jenny."

"Dinah, let's go," Preston said, and strode toward the door.

With Jenny held tightly in Dinah's arms, Preston sped away from the house.

"This is all my fault," he said, smacking the steering wheel with his hand. "I should have paid more attention when you said she felt warm and hadn't wanted her dinner. Dammit, why didn't I stop and think?"

"Preston, you had no way of knowing that—"

"All my fault," he repeated. He stopped at a red light and placed one hand gently on Jenny's head. "I'm sorry, Munchkin," he said softly. "I'm just so damn sorry!"

Nine

When Dinah and Preston swept through the doors of the emergency entrance at the hospital, a young woman in a nurse's cap and a young man wearing white rushed toward them, pushing a gurney between them.

"Hello, Dr. Harper," the nurse said. "We'll take Jenny. Dr. O'Leary arrived at the hospital just a minute ago."

"Fine," Preston said. He turned to Dinah, who was still holding Jenny. "Dinah, I'll put Jenny on the gurney."

He reached for the baby, but Dinah tightened her hold on Jenny. She stared at Preston, fear radiating from her eyes.

"No," she whispered. "I can't . . . I won't . . . I'll

take care of her. I'll read every single page in my book. Don't make me give her to those people, Preston. Please? Please?"

"Dinah," he said gently, "I know this is frightening, but we've got to get Jenny the care she needs. Maggie O'Leary is the finest in her field, believe me. Give me Jenny. Trust me, Dinah. I love you, and I love Jenny, you know that."

Yes, that was true, Dinah thought foggily. Preston loved Dinah. Preston loved Jenny. Oh, how he loved Jenny. It was possible, in fact, that Preston loved Jenny more than he loved Dinah, because he'd never asked Dinah to marry him and— Should she be thinking about that now? No, no, this wasn't the time. She had to concentrate on Jenny, do what was best for her precious baby.

"Dinah?" Preston said.

"Yes, all right," she said, fighting against threatening tears. "Yes."

He took Jenny from her and placed the baby on the gurney. Jenny began to cry. Two tears slid down Dinah's cheeks.

"Let's move," the man in white said.

Moments later the gurney disappeared through double green doors. Preston spoke to the nurse at the admitting desk while Dinah stood statue still, her gaze fixed on the doors that had swallowed up Jenny.

"We can wait for Maggie in her office," Preston said, returning to Dinah.

"Can't we go in there with Jenny?"

"We'd just be in the way at this point." He took a deep breath and let it out slowly. "Come on, let's go upstairs to Maggie's office."

The office they entered on the second floor was small but nicely decorated. There was a desk, a filing cabinet, and two pale blue easy chairs in front of the desk. An oil painting of rolling green hills hung on one wall, and a jaunty ceramic leprechaun sat on the edge of the desk.

Preston pulled off his bow tie and stuffed it into his pocket, then undid the top stud of his shirt. Dinah sank onto one of the blue chairs. She watched as Preston crossed the room to stare out the window at the glittering lights of the city.

"I should have paid more attention to what you were telling me about Jenny before we went to the dance," he said. "I know she's prone to ear infections. Dammit, why didn't I pay attention?"

"Preston, you did listen to me. You had no way of knowing this was going to happen. She was fine when we left her."

"She was warm. The fever was starting."

"She could just as easily have been warm from her bath, as you said. Clancy is a nurse. She didn't realize there was anything wrong either. None of us had any way of predicting that something this serious was going to happen."

He pounded the window frame with his fist. "I

was too hasty, didn't think it through like I should have. I—"

The door to the office opened and a woman entered. Preston spun around as Dinah got to her feet.

What a stunning woman, Dinah thought absently. She was tall, probably five eight or nine, and dark auburn curls tumbled wildly to her shoulders. Her eyes were large, the color of warm chocolate, and were framed in long lashes. Her features were classically lovely, and her figure was beautifully proportioned. She was wearing a floor-length green evening dress, the silky fabric changing colors as she moved.

"Hello, Preston," she said, then looked at Dinah. "You must be Dinah Bradshaw. I'm Maggie O'Leary. I saw you at the dance, but didn't get a chance to meet you in that mob. Look at the three of us. We're surely giving this drab old place a touch of class. It's a real pleasure to meet you, Dinah."

"Thank you," Dinah said. "How's Jenny?"

"Well, you did the right thing by rushing her here. Preston, we're looking at cholesteatoma."

"Dammit!" Preston swore.

"What's that?" Dinah asked fearfully.

"Let me explain," Maggie said. "That big fancy word means that Jenny has a fatty growth in her middle ear caused by chronic ear infections. I'm going to go in and remove the growth and repair any damage that's been done."

"You're—you're going to operate on her ear?"

"That's our only choice," Maggie said. "If all goes well, she'll be as good as new. But I'll be honest with you. There's a chance that she could be rendered deaf in that ear, depending on what I find when I go in."

Preston shrugged out of his tuxedo jacket. "I'll scrub."

"No, you won't, Preston!" Maggie said sternly. "You're not going in that operating room."

"The hell I'm not," he said none too quietly. "I can't assist, I'm not a surgeon, but I'm Jenny's pediatrician, and I'm qualified to be in that operating room."

"No," Maggie said, planting her hands on her hips.

"Dammit, Maggie," he said, his voice starting to quiver, "that's my daughter, my baby. Can't you understand that? I have to be with her. I love her, Maggie. It's my fault that this happened to her. I've got to be with Jenny."

"You'll be listening to me, you will, Harper," Maggie said, an Irish brogue suddenly evident in her speech. "This was *not* your fault. That tumor has been building over the months, and you know that to be true. You're *not* going in that operating room for the very reasons you'd be yelling at me about. Jenny is your daughter, your blessed wee one, and you're too emotionally involved. Now, you stay here with Dinah, where you belong, or I swear I'll deck you cold. Are you hearing me, Harper?"

"Damn you, O'Leary!" he yelled.

"Good. You heard me then. Sit down, shut up, and don't be giving me any more trouble. I'm the best there is, Preston Harper, and Jenny is in my hands now. It was surely lovely to meet you, Dinah, and may the saints be with you when you marry this stubborn man." She turned and started toward the door.

"Maggie!" Preston called.

She stopped and looked back at him. "You know you've pushed me too far when my brogue takes over. You're skating on ice that's thin for sure, Harper."

"I love Jenny," he said quietly. "She's the most important thing in my life."

"Preston," she said gently, "do you think I can't tell that? Of course you love your girl, both you and Dinah do. That's what it's all about. Now, let me get on with fixing your Munchkin as good as new. There'll be a leprechaun on my shoulder, never fear." She left the room and closed the door gently behind her.

Preston started after her, then stopped. His shoulders slumped, and he sank onto one of the blue chairs. Resting his elbows on his knees, he covered his face with his hands.

Dinah stared at him, her heart racing as Preston's passionately spoken words echoed in her mind.

That's my daughter, my baby. I love her. . . . She's the most important thing in my life . . . most important . . . most important . . .

Tears blurred Dinah's vision. Oh, dear heaven, she thought, what she'd feared was true. What she'd refused to dwell on had been brought into chilling reality by words that had seemed to be torn from Preston's very soul.

The most important thing in Preston's life was Jenny. She was his focus, his deepest love.

Dinah was second place, second choice, and that wasn't enough. That wasn't a solid foundation on which to build a future.

And, oh, how it hurt.

"Oh, God," Preston murmured, bringing Dinah from her tormented reverie.

His shoulders began to shake and a moan rumbled from his chest. He was crying.

She pressed trembling fingers to her lips to stifle a sob, then drew a steadying breath.

This was not the time, she told herself, to turn her attention inward to her shattering heart. The man she loved was suffering. The anguish was theirs to share together, because they both loved Jenny. This wasn't the time to think of the future beyond the next slow tick of the clock.

She crossed the room and dropped to her knees

beside Preston, placing one hand on his upper arm. Tears filled her eyes as Preston sobbed.

"My fault," he mumbled into his hands. "I failed Jenny as a doctor, as her father. Never should have gone to that dance. Her fever had started, and I left her. Love her so much. So sorry . . . so sorry, Jenny."

"Oh, Preston, don't do this to yourself," Dinah said, her voice strained with pain. "You heard Maggie. It's not your fault. You're a wonderful doctor, and a wonderful father too. I know—I know how much you love Jenny, Preston."

He dropped his hands and looked at her, tears tracking his cheeks and shimmering in his dark eyes. His face had a gray pallor beneath his tan.

"Do you?" he asked. "Do you really know how much I love Jenny?"

"Yes," she said, forcing the word past the sob that caught in her throat.

He gripped one of her hands and strove to bring his emotions under control. Drawing a shuddering breath, he gazed at Dinah.

"I love you," he said. "I'm falling apart and you're being strong for both of us." He stood, helping her to her feet, then pulled her tightly to him. "Lord, how I love you."

But not enough, Dinah thought in anguish.

"When this nightmare is over," he went on, "we'll . . . no, this isn't the time to talk about that. We've got to concentrate on Jenny."

When this nightmare was over, she thought, she would have no choice but to walk out of Preston's life. To take Jenny and go.

"Jenny's going to be fine, you'll see," he said. "Our girl will be as good as new. This operation won't keep our Munchkin down for long. No, sir, not our Jenny. She'll be destroying everything in our house again in no time."

It was suddenly all too much. Dinah felt as though she were being physically beaten by Preston's words. *Our* girl . . . *our* Munchkin . . . *our* Jenny . . . *our* house.

No!

Jenny would be Dinah's, hers alone. Dear Lord, she couldn't breathe; she was suffocating under the weight of fear for Jenny and what was happening in that operating room. And from the crushing mass of broken dreams and shattered hopes for a glorious future with Preston.

"Our Jenny will be walking soon," he was saying. "We'll have to put a baby gate across the stairs so that she doesn't—"

"Stop it!" Dinah screamed. She wrenched herself out of his embrace and stepped back, fresh tears spilling onto her cheeks. "Please, don't do this anymore. I'm so worried about Jenny and I can't deal with it, not now. You keep going on and on. . . . Don't say another word. Don't do this to me."

He frowned, obviously confused. "What's wrong?

I don't understand what you're talking about. What have I done?"

"You've come to love a precious, beautiful baby," she said, trying to control her sobs, "as though she were your own daughter. She stole your heart. No, you gave it to her gladly, all of it. You're a rare and wonderful man, Preston, to love Jenny so totally, so unconditionally."

"But you're upset. I don't—"

"Oh, God, Preston, don't you see? It won't work for us. I heard what you said. You said that Jenny is the most important thing in your life."

"Wait a minute. Dinah—"

"No," she said, shaking her head, "let me finish. I believe that you love me, Preston, but you don't love me enough. You don't really want a wife, you want only a baby . . . Jenny. You speak of a future centered on her, not us. You're committed to her, not me. I'm part of the picture only because Jenny is mine."

"No!"

"Dear Lord, Preston, you haven't asked me to marry you, be your wife, your partner, your best friend. Yes, you love me, but I'm second choice, an afterthought. It's not enough, don't you realize that? I can't live with you, knowing that if it weren't for Jenny I wouldn't be wanted there at all. Jenny is not *ours*, Preston, she's *mine*, and when she's better, I'm taking her back to my apartment to raise her as *my* daughter . . . alone."

Preston shook his head, expressions of shock and disbelief on his face. "No. Dinah, you've got this all wrong. You don't understand."

She wrapped her arms around herself as a shiver coursed through her. "Yes, I do," she said quietly, wearily. "I understand perfectly. It's not your fault, it's just the way it is. I had such hopes, dreams. . . . But I can't live this way."

"I've made such a mess of this," he said, dragging one hand through his hair. "Dinah, please, listen to me. In my mind, heart, and soul, we *are* married, you're my wife. When I said that Jenny was the most important thing in my life, I was speaking as a father. As a man, I put *you* first."

"No."

"Yes. Dinah, I haven't asked you to marry me because I was scared to death you'd refuse."

Her eyes widened. "What?"

"So much has happened to you so quickly, I was afraid you'd want to wait, have more proof that we could manage our careers, Jenny, and have it all, together. I was so terrified of hearing you say no that I kept postponing asking you. Oh, Dinah, the thought of losing you is more than I can handle. I don't want to go through the rest of my life without you. Yes, I love Jenny as my daughter, a daughter who will grow up and leave to find her place in the world. But you and I are forever, until death parts us."

"Preston?"

"Please, Dinah, please, don't sentence me to a cold, empty existence without you. I love you so damn much. I need you, with me, as my wife, my other half. Dinah"—his voice choked with emotion —"*please.*"

"Oh, Preston," she whispered.

"You were never second choice, Dinah." He drew a ragged breath. "I was loving you with all that I am. Loving you, loving Jenny. I failed Jenny, and somehow I failed you, too, or you would have believed in that love, trusted in that love. I'm sorry. I—" He shook his head as his emotions overwhelmed him, making it impossible to speak.

She suddenly flung herself against him with such force, he staggered as he instinctively wrapped his arms around her.

"Oh, Preston, forgive me," she said. "I was terribly wrong. But I was so hurt, so filled with pain because I love you so very, very much and I thought . . . oh, please forgive me for doubting you. I want to spend the rest of my life with you, with Jenny, with our other children. Oh, Preston, *please.*"

"I love you, Dinah. I swear to God that I love you first. *You* are the most important thing in my life when I am being just a man, not a father."

"Yes, yes, I know that now. I love you."

"Dinah Bradshaw, will you marry me?"

"Oh, yes, Preston Harper, just as quickly as possible."

He kissed her, their tears mingling as their lips

met. It was a kiss of forgiveness, of greater under-standing, of commitment renewed. It was a kiss of love.

Then slowly, reluctantly, they ended the sweet embrace, moved the chairs together, and sat down, hands entwined.

And they waited.

Two hours later Maggie O'Leary burst in the door, wearing surgical greens and a big smile. Dinah and Preston were instantly on their feet.

"Oh, bless the leprechauns," Maggie said, beam-ing, "I'm a brilliant surgeon. A genius at thirty years old. Your Jenny is absolutely fine. I removed the growth, repaired the damage to the inner ear, and checked her hearing on my fancy machines while she snoozed. Perfect. She can go home in about three days, four at the most."

Preston strode across the room and hugged Maggie until she begged for mercy.

"Take him out of here, Dinah," Maggie said, laughing. "Have a peek at your sleeping Jenny, then go home and get some rest. You both look awful, if you don't mind my saying so. Jenny and I are gorgeous, but you two are grim."

"I don't know how to thank you," Dinah said.

"Just be happy," Maggie said, "and love your darling Munchkin."

"Guaranteed," Preston said. He gathered up their belongings, and with Dinah close to his side, left the room. "I love ya, O'Leary," he called over his shoulder.

"You're full of blarney, Harper," she answered, then she sighed. "And you're a lucky lass, little Jenny," she said softly.

Dinah walked her fingers up Preston's bare chest and snuggled closer to him in the big bed. "Preston?"

"Mmm," he said, not opening his eyes.

"Are you asleep?"

"I'm a sexually sated, contented man, who's *trying* to sleep."

"Oh." She paused. "Don't you think that Jenny is doing beautifully, considering she had surgery a month ago?"

He still didn't open his eyes. "Jenny has learned to walk. Jenny is exhausting. Jenny is a menace to society."

Dinah laughed softly. "And tomorrow we have twin four-year-old boys coming to spend the day so they can look us over and decide if they like us."

"Yes. Go to sleep. I love you, Mrs. Harper."

"I love you too, Mr. Harper."

"Good."

"Preston?"

"I'm sleeping, Dinah."

"Just one more teeny-tiny question, okay?"

"Mmm."

"Preston, what was in that giant acorn you and your chipmunk friend found?"

Preston burst into laughter as he opened his eyes and scooped Dinah into his arms. He settled her on top of his naked body, then wove his fingers through her silken hair and brought her mouth down to his.

Chipmunks and giant acorns were quickly forgotten. . . .

THE EDITOR'S CORNER

Next month you have even more wonderful reading to look forward to from LOVESWEPT. We're publishing another four of our most-asked-for books as Silver Signature Editions, which as you know are some of the best romances from our early days! In this group you'll find **ONCE IN A BLUE MOON** (#26) by Billie Green, **SEND NO FLOWERS** (#51) by Sandra Brown, and two interrelated books—**CAPTURE THE RAINBOW** and **TOUCH THE HORIZON** by Iris Johansen. Those of you who haven't had the pleasure of savoring these scrumptious stories are in for one bountiful feast! But do leave room on your reading menu for our six new LOVESWEPTs, because they, too, are gourmet delights!

A new Iris Johansen book is always something to celebrate, and Iris provides you with a real gem next month. **TENDER SAVAGE,** LOVESWEPT #420, is the love story of charismatic revolutionary leader Ricardo Lazaro and daring Lara Clavel. Determined to free the man who saved her brother's life, Lara risks her own life in a desperate plan that takes a passionate turn. Trapped with Ricardo in his cramped jail cell, Lara intends to playact a seduction to fool their jailer—but instead she discovers a savage need to be possessed, body and soul, by her freedom fighter. Lara knew she was putting herself in jeopardy, but she didn't expect the worst danger to be her overwhelming feelings for the rebel leader of the Caribbean island. Iris is a master at developing tension between strong characters, and placing them in a cell together is one sure way to ignite those incendiary sparks. Enjoy **TENDER SAVAGE,** it's vintage Johansen.

Every so often a new writer comes along whose work seems custom-made for LOVESWEPT. We feel Patricia Burroughs is such a writer. Patricia's first LOVESWEPT is **SOME ENCHANTED SEASON,** #421, and in it she offers readers the very best of what you've come to expect in our romances—humor, tender emotion, sparkling dialogue, smoldering sensuality, carefully crafted prose, and characters who tug at your heart. When artist Kevyn Llewellyn spots the man who is the epitome of the warrior-god she has to paint, she can't believe her good fortune. But convincing him to pose for her is another story. Rusty Rivers thinks the lady with the silver-streaked hair is a kook, but he's irresistibly drawn to her nonetheless. An incredible tease, Rusty tells her she can use his body only if he can use hers! Kevyn can't

(continued)

deal with his steamy embraces and fiery kisses, she's always felt so isolated and alone. The last thing she wants in her life is a hunk with a wicked grin. But, of course, Rusty is too much a hero to take no for an answer! This story is appealing on so many levels, you'll be captivated from page one.

If Janet Evanovich weren't such a dedicated writer, I think she could have had a meteoric career as a comedienne. Her books make me laugh until I cry, and **WIFE FOR HIRE**, LOVESWEPT #422, is no exception. Hero Hank Mallone spotted trouble when Maggie Toone sat down and said she'd marry him. But Hank isn't one to run from a challenge, and having Maggie pretend to be his wife in order to improve his reputation seemed like the challenge of a lifetime. His only problem comes when he starts to falling in love with the tempting firecracker of a woman. Maggie never expected her employer to be drop-dead handsome or to be the image of every fantasy she'd ever had. Cupid really turns the tables on these two, and you won't want to miss a single minute of the fun!

Another wonderful writer makes her LOVESWEPT debut this month, and she fits into our lineup with grace and ease. Erica Spindler is a talented lady who has published several books for Silhouette under her own name. Her first LOVESWEPT, #423, is a charmingly fresh story called **RHYME OR REASON**. Heroine Alex Clare is a dreamer with eyes that sparkle like the crystal she wears as a talisman, and Dr. Walker Chadwick Ridgeman thinks he needs to have his head examined for being drawn to the lovely seductress. After all, he's a serious man who believes in what he can see, and Alex believes the most important things in life are those that you can't see or touch but only feel. Caught up in her sensual spell, Walker learns firsthand of the changes a magical love can bring about.

Judy Gill's next three books aren't part of a "series," but they will feature characters whose paths will cross. In **DREAM MAN**, LOVESWEPT #424, heroine Jeanie Leslie first meets Max McKenzie in her dreams. She'd conjured up the dashingly handsome hero as the answer to all her troubled sister's needs. But when he actually walks into her office one day in response to the intriguing ad she'd run, Jeanie knows without a doubt that she could never fix him up with her sister—because she wants him for herself! Max applies for the "Man Wanted" position out of curiosity, but once he sets eyes on Jeanie, he's suddenly compelled to convince

(continued)

her how right they are for each other. While previously neither would admit to wanting a permanent relationship, after they meet they can't seem to think about anything else. But it takes a brush with death to bring these two passionate lovers together forever!

Helen Mittermeyer closes the month with **FROZEN IDOL**, LOVESWEPT #425, the final book in her *Men of Ice* trilogy. If her title doesn't do it, her story will send a thrill down your spine over the romance between untouchable superstar Dolph Wakefield and smart and sexy businesswoman Bedelia Fronsby. Fate intervenes in Dolph's life when Bedelia shows up ten years after she'd vanished without a trace and left him to deal with the deepest feelings he'd ever had for a woman. Now the owner of a company that plans to finance Dolph's next film, Bedelia finds herself succumbing once again to the impossible Viking of a man whose power over her emotions has only strengthened with time. When Dolph learns the true reason she'd left him, he can't help but decide to cherish her always. Once again Helen delivers a story fans are sure to love!

In the upcoming months we will begin several unique promotions which we're certain will be hits with readers. Starting in October and continuing through January, you will be able to accumulate coupons from the backs of our books which you may redeem for special hardcover "Keepsake Editions" of LOVESWEPTs by your favorite authors. Watch for more information on how to save your coupons and where to send them.

Another innovative new feature we're planning to offer is a "900" number readers can use to reach LOVESWEPT by telephone. As soon as the line is set up, we'll let you know the number—until then, keep reading!

Sincerely,

Susann Brailey

Susann Brailey
Editor
LOVESWEPT
Bantam Books
666 Fifth Avenue
New York, NY 10103

FAN OF THE MONTH

Carollyn McCauley

After seeing the Fan of the Month in the backs of LOVESWEPTs, I wished that I'd have a chance to be one. I thought it would never happen. Due to a close friend and the people at LOVESWEPT, I got my wish granted.

I've been a reader of romance novels for twenty years, ever since I finished nursing school.

LOVESWEPTs arrive at the Waldenbooks store I go to around the first week of the month. Starting that week I haunt the store until the LOVESWEPTs are placed on the shelves, then, within two or three days, I've finished reading them and have to wait anxiously for the next month's shipment.

I have a few favorite authors: Iris Johansen, Kay Hooper, Billie Green, Sharon and Tom Curtis, and many more. As far as I'm concerned, the authors that LOVESWEPT chooses are the cream of the crop in romance. I encourage the readers of LOVESWEPT who buy books only by authors they've read before to let themselves go and take a chance on the new authors. They'll find they'll be pleasantly surprised and will never be disappointed. The books are well written, and the unusual and unique plots will capture their attention. From the first book in the line to the current ones, they have all held my attention from page one to the last, causing me to experience a variety of emotions and feelings.

Over the years of reading the different romances available, I've cut back on the amount I purchase due to the cost. LOVESWEPT has maintained such a high standard of quality that I'll always buy all six each month!

OFFICIAL RULES TO
LOVESWEPT'S
DREAM MAKER GIVEAWAY
(See entry card in center of this book)

1. NO PURCHASE NECESSARY. To enter both the sweepstakes and accept the risk-free trial offer, follow the directions published on the insert card in this book. Return your entry on the reply card provided. If you do not wish to take advantage of the risk-free trial offer, but wish to enter the sweepstakes, return the entry card only with the "FREE ENTRY" sticker attached, or send your name and address on a 3x5 card to : Loveswept Sweepstakes, Bantam Books, PO Box 985, Hicksville, NY 11802-9827.

2. To be eligible for the prizes offered, your entry must be received by September 17, 1990. We are not responsible for late, lost or misdirected mail. Winners will be selected on or about October 16, 1990 in a random drawing under the supervision of Marden Kane, Inc., an independent judging organization, and except for those prizes which will be awarded to the first 50 entrants, prizes will be awarded after that date. By entering this sweepstakes, each entrant accepts and agrees to be bound by these rules and the decision of the judges which shall be final and binding. This sweepstakes will be presented in conjunction with various book offers sponsored by Bantam Books under the following titles: Agatha Christie "Mystery Showcase", Louis L'Amour "Great American Getaway", Loveswept "Dreams Can Come True" and Loveswept "Dream Makers". Although the prize options and graphics of this Bantam Books sweepstakes will vary in each of these book offers, the value of each prize level will be approximately the same and prize winners will have the options of selecting any prize offered within the prize level won.

3. Prizes in the Loveswept "Dream Maker" sweepstakes: Grand Prize (1) 14 Day trip to either Hawaii, Europe or the Caribbean. Trip includes round trip air transportation from any major airport in the US and hotel accomodations (approximate retail value $6,000); Bonus Prize (1) $1,000 cash in addition to the trip; Second Prize (1) 27" Color TV (approximate retail value $900).

4. This sweepstakes is open to residents of the US, and Canada (excluding the province of Quebec), who are 18 years of age or older. Employees of Bantam Books, Bantam Doubleday Dell Publishing Group Inc., their affiliates and subsidiaries, Marden Kane Inc. and all other agencies and persons connected with conducting this sweepstakes and their immediate family members are not eligible to enter this sweepstakes. This offer is subject to all applicable laws and regulations and is void in the province of Quebec and wherever prohibited or restricted by law. In order to win a prize, residents of Canada will be required to correctly answer a time-limited arithmetical skill-testing question.

5. Winners will be notified by mail and will be required to execute an affidavit of eligibility and release which must be returned within 14 days of notification or an alternate winner will be selected. Prizes are not transferable. Trip prize must be taken within one year of notification and is subject to airline departure schedules and ticket and accommodation availability. Winner must have a valid passport. No substitution will be made for any prize except as offered. If a prize should be unavailable at sweepstakes end, sponsor reserves the right to substitute a prize of equal or greater value. Winners agree that the sponsor, its affiliates, and their agencies and employees shall not be liable for injury, loss or damage of any kind resulting from an entrant's participation in this offer or from the acceptance or use of the prizes awarded. Odds of winning are dependant upon the number of entries received. Taxes, if any, are the sole responsibility of the winners. Winner's entry and acceptance of any prize offered constitutes permission to use the winner's name, photograph or other likeness for purposes of advertising and promotion on behalf of Bantam Books and Bantam Doubleday Dell Publishing Group Inc. without additional compensation to the winner.

6. For a list of winners (available after 10/16/90), send a self addressed stamped envelope to Bantam Books Winners List, PO Box 704, Sayreville, NJ 08871.

7. The free gifts are available only to entrants who also agree to sample the Loveswept subscription program on the terms described. The sweepstakes prizes offered by affixing the "Free Entry" sticker to the Entry Form are available to all entrants, whether or not an entrant chooses to affix the "Free Books" sticker to the Entry Form.